THE FOLKESTONE ANTHOLOGY 2013

FOLKESTONE WRITERS

THE

FOLKESTONE

ANTHOLOGY

2013

STORIES IN PROSE AND VERSE

EDITED BY JOHN SUSSAMS

Published by John Sussams
for Folkestone Writers
www.folkestonewriterspress.com

All copyright remains with the original authors.

All rights reserved. No part of this book may be reproduced or stored in an information retrieval system (other than for purposes of review) without prior written permission of the copyright holders.

First Edition November 2013

ISBN 978-0-9551 952-4-2

To order additional copies of this book please contact the Editor
(john@sussams.freeserve.co.uk)

Cover design: John Sussams

Printed and bound by Orbital Print Ltd
www.orbitalprint.co.uk

CONTENTS

Sugar and Spice	Frances Addison	1
First Impressions	Bob Brown	5
The Archer	Peter Burgess	11
The Quarry	Helen Derry	20
The Victim	Helen Derry	26
An Education	Grant Gibson	31
Blackout	Tim Goss	45
Joey's	Penny Gotch	64
A Fireside Tale	Margaret Harland-Suddes	68
The Afterlife of Stephen Balls	Briony Kapoor	82
The Bike	Lisamarie Lamb	87
Time Shadows	Sue Peake	90
Waiting	Sue Peake	95
Centring the Olives	Michele Sheldon	98
The Mantelpiece	Michele Sheldon	108
Stiff Upper Lip	Nick Spurrier	116
The Ruined Mill	John Sussams	124
Electronic Warfare	Alexander Tulloch	130
The Visitor	Alexander Tulloch	136
Tell him Now	Mike Umbers	143
Her New Gatepost	Mike Umbers	149

SUGAR AND SPICE

Fran Addison

'Amen' Frankie mumbles, working at the wafer, dry as cardboard with her tongue. Load of old rubbish. Pairs of feet creak back and forth along the altar rail. The cup touches her lips. She rolls the drop of sweet wine around her mouth and slouches back to her place.

Not long to go.

'Are you catching the bus?' Gina hisses in her ear. 'What did you tell your mum?'

'What we said,' Frankie raises her voice a notch, 'Julie's we said, straight after dinner.' *Go in Peace to Love and Serve the Lord.* They scramble along the pew straining towards the door and the sunshine and The Plan.

The righteous tut and scowl at them.

'Silly old buggers.' Gina grins.

Frankie is in the kitchen, doing the washing up. It's almost two o'clock, the afternoon is slipping away.

'Shall I pour this gravy away Mum?'

'Don't you go pouring anything away, we're not made of money. And stop clattering about'

'Billy keeps running his car over my feet.'

'Give me a bit of peace Francine, let me drink my tea. Billy outside with that, there's a good boy.'

'Flippin' heck.' Frankie drops the gravy boat. 'Flippin' hell.'

'What's the matter with you?' Mum stubs out her cigarette and slaps Frankie's arm. 'Mind your language lady. I can do without your moods. Lucky for you that didn't break.'

'Sorry mum, I'm late. I'm worried about my exams. I've got to get over to Julie's quick.'

'I don't see why she has to go all the way over there to do her revising.' Frankie's dad opens the door for Billy.

'Her father's an optician Ken. They're a clever lot.'

Gina meets Frankie at the bus station. 'I've been waiting ages.'

'Yeah, alright for you, I had to do the sodding washing up.' They spend the afternoon on the beach chucking pebbles at the sea. Around five Frankie fishes a small magnifying mirror out of her bag, squints at her reflection and starts layering on *Pan-Stick*, extra thick over the spots on her forehead under her fringe. She spits onto a block of mascara, works up a thick coating on the brush and spikes up her eyelashes, stopping now and again to wipe blobs from her cheek.

'*Coral Shimmer?*' Gina asks, picking through a selection of lipsticks.

'How do I look?'

'Really nice.'

They head off to The Rotunda to look for Don and Stephen. They find them whacking a pin-ball machine.

'Awright.'

'Yeah.'

The girls perch on the side of a kiddy car. They sniff and gaze out of the window, make minute adjustments to their hair. Time passes.

'Paul's my favourite, he's fab.' Gina says.

'Really? I love George. John next.'

'What about Ringo?'

'Yuk.'

The boys, backs turned, keep pinging away at the machine. 'Ohh, Paul, John, we love you. Bleedin' Beatles. Bleedin' nancies. Stones, right mate?' Don says.

'Yeah the Stones. Right.'

Frankie's head is spinning. She watches a puddle of beer snake across the table towards her and begin to drip down onto the floor. She shifts her feet. On the jukebox Dusty's pleading: *I just don't know what to do with myself.*

Frankie's had three gin and oranges. Don has his hand clamped on her thigh. 'Let's go outside,' he says, breathing beer and smoke into her ear.

'If you like.' She hopes she won't be sick.

Gina winks. 'We're going to the bogs,' she says. She pulls Frankie up and they weave through the crowded lounge bar to the ladies. Frankie pushes the door open, walks in and slumps against the sink. 'I don't feel very well.'

'Get up Frankie,' Gina says, 'get up quick or they'll go off and leave us.'

'Don won't go off. He paid for my drinks.'

'We haven't got long, last bus goes at half-past. Here, dab some water on your face.'

Don and Frankie wrestle in a narrow alley-way behind the Odeon. It's dark. He has her pressed up against the wall and she wonders what she's standing in and if the back of her jumper's getting dirty. He's got one hand inside her bra, pummelling her breasts, the other struggles to find a way up her skirt and through her knickers. She keeps her legs crossed and pushes his hand away.

'Come on Frankie.'

She's worrying about the time; I'll be in for it if I'm late. 'I've got to go now.' He's panting; slack jawed, wet lips on her neck. They struggle on.

'My bus goes at half past.'

He grips her hand, rubs it on his cock.
'I've got to go now.' She's had enough.
'You're a right teaser you.'
Don gives up and walks to the end of the alley. He turns silhouetted under a street lamp, fumbling for a cigarette. He stares at her. She watches him. He won't go with me again. I don't care. He flicks the match on the ground and walks off shouting 'Frankie Andrews. Bleedin' prick teaser.'
Frankie pulls her skirt straight, smoothes her hair and runs up to the bus station. Gina is already onboard, beckoning from the back window.
'Did you do it?'
'Course.'

——ooOoo——

Fran Addison graduated in English and American Literature with Creative Writing in 2009. Recently retired from her job as an administrator with the Adult Education Service, she intends to sit by her beach hut with a couple of sharp pencils and a jumbo pad and get started on a novel.

FIRST IMPRESSIONS

Bob Brown

'Gosh, what a hunk, alpha-male first class and no mistake,' Amanda thought as she stood in the doorway of the gallery's latest exhibition of abstract expressionism by unknown artists. It was the first night launch and she slowly sipped her complimentary wine. Being in Chelsea she had expected a decent tipple and the Grand Cru had just the right hint of minerals beneath its floral bouquet; to ensure she was not disappointed. The quality of the refreshment she had anticipated, such a delicious man she had not. From her vantage point, she gazed at the tall Adonis. He was studying a large and colourful painting. His attitude was obviously disapproving and she was not surprised; from where she stood it appeared simply hideous. He definitely looked like someone she would want to meet. His reefer blazer looked expensive and at odds with the cargo chinos and trekker boots, however, the athletic frame on which they hung would certainly pass muster. Something about attractive people enables them to carry off any outfit, however incongruous. She moved up closer for a better view. Azure blue eyes under a shock of blond hair cut in public school fashion. The noble jaw, strong mouth and high cheekbones completed the highborn look. From the proud way he held his head he looked like a latter day Tolkien prince fresh in from Middle Earth.

Amanda was impressed – and she was not easily impressed. At thirty, she was running her own interior design business and prided herself on her ability to read people. It also gave her great confidence and the fierce determination to get what she wanted. She had a distinct image of her ideal man – a muscular powerhouse that concealed a seething animal passion laced with charm. Most importantly, he had to be her intellectual equal. It was true she had high requirements but, after all, she was worth it, wasn't she? She was certainly no mean catch herself with her flaming red hair, large green eyes and generous lips. Together with her captivating figure, these attributes ensured there was never a shortage of potential suitors. There were many handsome men in the circles within which she moved. Not all of them were married either. But the ones who made advances to her never seemed to match her keen-witted adversarial skills. She wanted a mental sparring partner as well as a physical one. So whenever playing the dating game Amanda had decided to control the situation by being the one to make the first move when it came to flirting. That way she could guarantee to gauge the suitability of prospective partners by setting little tests in the opening banter.

  The one drawback to this avant-garde approach was that she might somehow fail to maintain her tactical advantage in the mind games which inevitably followed the initial contact. When a man makes advances, the lady can choose to remain aloof or act coy should the encounter not be not to her liking. However, as she was the one making the running it was for her to keep the verbal foreplay on track until the necessary judgements were made. The golden rule in both her business and personal life was that first impressions were of paramount importance; and so appearing foolish was her greatest fear. Although this was her Achilles heel she seldom had cause to worry, as most men she met couldn't wait to fall over themselves trying to impress her, and invariably assumed the role of fool in the process.

  Amanda levelled her cool gaze once again upon the good-looking stranger.

  'Yes,' she speculated, 'this one is worth trying out.'

  She quickly ran through in her mind how she would begin the play. Her regular game plan for such occasions was tried and true, and mastered to perfection. To begin, she would break the ice by making an innocuous remark; a comment on that monstrosity of a painting would do the trick. This would be followed up by demonstrating how conversant she was with the subject of art. She knew his responses to this approach would provide adequate opportunity to check out his appreciation of what she deemed to be the finer things in life. If her initial reaction to him was favourable then she would ascertain his availability and, if it still felt right, go for the main chance and invite him to join her for a drink in that fashionable little wine bar she had spotted on the corner of the street. Amanda usually ratified her initial judgements in such places as bars or restaurants. She found she could tell almost as much about someone from observing how they interacted with bar-staff and waiters as she could from how they related to her; often true colours would flourish when not directly under the spotlight. She complimented herself on the breadth and temerity of her plan and chuckled quietly as she thought to herself,

'All that can come later; first of all he has to pass the aptitude test.'

Amanda crossed the short space between them discretely; a casual onlooker would never guess her intent as she gracefully circled and then descended upon her prey.

'What an unusual painting, I wonder exactly what it was the artist was trying to convey,' she pouted from behind his shoulder.

The man turned and settled a critical gaze upon her. At once his look changed, a warm smile spreading across his lips and an inviting sparkle springing to life in his eyes.

'Ah good, he's hooked,' Amanda thought knowingly.

'Does it look strange to you too?' he responded to her opening gambit.

Amanda coolly examined the abstract work before her, hesitating just long enough for him to fully appreciate her classic good looks in profile.

'Rather strong use of contrast' she mused. Now was the time to test him. 'The shape is a bit organic but I'm lost on the movement style, any ideas?' she cunningly asked.

The man thought carefully. 'Clearly it's from the school of painful hangovers on a Sunday morning' he answered with feigned affectedness.

They held each other's stare momentarily before bursting out in simultaneous laughter that was quickly stifled as they became aware of the turning heads of people around them. Giggling softly like conspirators they moved closer together. He held out his hand.

'Tyler Elliot' he said affably.

'Amanda Jessup' she responded as she shook his hand.

The lightweight seduction attempt was going well and Amanda decided to pursue her clandestine inquiry into his critical acumen. She noticed the peevish way he was peering once more at the painting.

'Whatever was going on in the artist's head to combine such earthy use of colour with those subtle classical lines … some kind of riddle perhaps?' she commented wryly.

She watched him as he carefully pondered her question.

'Yes, it certainly looks a bit weird hanging there like that,' he replied pensively. 'It is impossible to see what the artist was trying to convey,' he added conclusively.

She appraised him swiftly. Yes, he had that certain something but was he free and single? Amanda's principle was to cut to the chase when it came to the rules of engagement; her time was too precious to waste on a hopeless cause. With measured indifference she enquired in her most nonchalant tone, 'Do you have to rush off anywhere … Is there someone waiting for you?'

Tyler faced her openly and with undisguised candour answered her unspoken question by turning her tactical inquisitiveness into his own challenge for her. 'I have made a study of this type of art and believe I know what is wrong about this picture. If you can tell me exactly why it's jarring on you, too then I will be yours to command for this evening.'

Bathing in the radiance of his unflinching gaze something inside her melted, she felt her legs might not support her as a giant butterfly in her stomach began to stir excitedly. Suddenly, somehow, the stakes of the game had risen and she needed to get to know this man better. 'Maybe we could discuss it over a cocktail?' she offered hopefully, for the first time hesitation creeping into her polished demeanour. Drat that flapping butterfly.

He scrutinised her with calm assurance. 'You're not getting off the hook that easily. In my experience, how someone evaluates art is the same as how they see life. If you want me …' (he hesitated to give Amanda a chance to be outraged, should he have overstepped the mark) '… for me to take you to dinner you will have to convince me you love art as much as I do.' He looked at her expectantly.

An age seemed to go by as Amanda panicked inwardly. What did this mean? Was he an art critic trying to catch her out? Was he playing her at her own game, testing her character as she had planned to test his? Was he merely toying with her? This was the one possibility that had stifled her innate reflex to cut him down for his audacity. Could he actually be the equal for which she searched so tirelessly? It galled her to think that she, the one who commanded the play at all times, might not appear worthy enough in his eyes. Had the hunter become the hunted? 'Think, think, think,' she repeated to herself. She must not appear inept at describing why she thought the picture was such a disaster. Her biggest fear of failing to make a good first impression surfaced like a mocking Nemesis that threatened to tarnish her carefully cultivated air of sophistication. That was not going to happen. She would have to demonstrate her adeptness at art critique.

Amanda refocused her attention on the picture, took a deep breath and, in her best descriptive manner, delivered with authority her considered opinion. 'The saturation of colour is juvenile. The swirling mood those waves create are at odds with the subtle delicacies of the finer forms. The monumental elongation is so alien in significance that one can only conclude the artist was having a real bad day'

Tyler clapped his hands with spontaneous glee. 'How simply wonderful,' he beamed appreciatively, 'I concur wholeheartedly with your conclusion, it's exactly what I was thinking the moment you came in.' He went on to add, 'It will be my undoubted pleasure to take you somewhere that befits such magnificent powers of observation'.

Amanda's joy was boundless; she had passed the test and won a very intriguing prize. Would it be romantic Italian or perhaps an intimate French bistro? Whatever, to the victor the spoils. Her heart was pounding as she bathed in his admiring gaze. She could not stop herself adding the piece de résistance that would underscore her undoubted prowess at critical perception. 'In my business first impressions count. However, I have to say that whoever concocted this visual travesty had not spared a thought for the dire effect it would instantly have upon the viewer's sensibilities. I wonder what kind of poor tortured soul evoked this dreadful apparition,' she speculated unkindly. 'Would you care to add anything?' she playfully continued, having so comprehensively assassinated any artistic merit the painting might have possessed.

'Yes' said Tyler, 'It is definitely hung upside down.'

'How can you be so sure?" Amanda purred, basking in the glow of her anticipated triumph. 'I am the artist,' replied Tyler dryly. 'Fancy a cheese sandwich?'

——ooOoo——

Bob Brown worked in telecommunications for 30 years before changing direction to study holistic health. Since 2006 he has practised the healing art of Reiki as a therapist and subsequently as a teacher based in Folkestone. He completed a Creative Writing course at South Kent College in 2004 which covered feature articles, short stories, film scripts, expressive prose and poetry. He is currently working on a self-help book which he hopes to complete in the near future.

THE ARCHER

Peter Burgess

Were I to tell you my name now, the thunder of it would deafen you to the subtleties of my tale, and much of the smack and sting would go from the lesson I must teach you. Know only that I had a reputation second to none here in Europe as the finest archer yet sired by God on all the bloody wars and tournaments of the five centuries since Charlemagne roused Christendom against the Mongol armies. And since I had been most generous in my gift of arrows to those men from Hell you may well measure my discontent at the sound of our own women rumouring of yet greater prowess in archery, in some remote and barbarous province of the East.

"The Men of the East" - I choke on that appellation! Chatterers are always putting the proof of their silly stories away beyond what can be seen and fixed with facts. This supreme skill in bowmanship I had not seen much evidenced, my ladies, in the gory field so foreign to your weaker nature, nor had I heard any such claim in the wonderful cacophony of the dying enemy's screams. None the less, the very keen and inquiescent hunger for the mark that removed me from the common crowd now drove me to quit that familiar hubbub, to prove myself directly.

I set out to find these fabled archers, first into the enemy-infested provinces to the East of our stronghold - no, I was never far from the chafing limits of power! - into mountains where I knew not one instant of safety, so close to survival's edge did I run. But there is no armour that can turn an arrow shot from a longbow pulled to its full extent, and there is no bird nor anything in Creation that flies more swiftly or more true.

At last, at the end of months, I came to a land so far from my battlefields that those wars I had left behind were only rumours, and the inhabitants no friends to my restless and destructive enemy which had ravaged them too, ranging Eastward before gathering strength to storm forth against the unknown West. But here, according to the fables I had heard, the Mongol armies had found amongst these quiet people archers of such amazing skill that they did not even take aim before unleashing their shafts.

I quickly learned that it was well thought of not to boast of such art, and the men I sought were not to be found. Nevertheless, one who did have fame was Yun-Pi, the teacher of archers, currently rumoured to be finishing with his last pupil.

A man of utmost resolution, Yun-Pi devoted himself to training night and day. It was therefore impossible to see him except at such a time as I had chanced upon. He dwelt on the Plateau Of Blue Grass high in the Tingtze mountains, and as I made my way there it struck me that if he were indeed the legend to whom the greatest bowmen owed their unanswerable fame, then why should I not be his next student?

The Plateau of Blue Grass was a wild and inhospitable place. The grass, what little of it sprung up between the rocks of that high, desolate spot, did indeed display a strange, bluish glitter. It was a blustery day, and an icy wind thrashed the plateau. The very rocks creaked against one another in the gale, their ancient complaint much like that of the bending yew of a long-bow, and sudden gusts ripping through the isolated clumps of long grass sounded to my ear like the wild and terrible whisper of the loosed arrow as it hurtles towards its victim.

I saw Yun-Pi almost immediately. It must have been him, because the whole of the plateau floor was in my view as I descended, and nobody else was in sight. A small figure dressed in the traditional black robe of the teacher, he was facing me, apparently unsurprised by my arrival. As I approached I could see he was staring at me, expressionless except for a slight twinkle in the eye.

The weather was bad enough to make me grit my teeth against the chill. Before I had even reached him I was in no doubt as to his venerable status, for he stood there oblivious to the conditions in which he chose to spend his life. The closer I came to him, the more I gained an accurate estimate of his size, finally realising that he was an exceedingly diminutive figure. I bowed, but feeling that this did not put me appreciably below his eyes, I resorted to kneeling before him on the sharp, broken stones.

He chose not to speak. From my position of abasement, I recited to him the valorous aspects of my expedition and how I had come from the other side of the world to kneel at his feet and to learn from him; how notwithstanding my reputation as the finest archer under the stars I had always known that I had more to learn; and that finally how, in the pure love of this art to which I had dedicated my life, I had resolved to risk all to come here and attempt to perfect my skill. He listened to this but did not seem overly impressed; for when I looked up the twinkle had gone from his eye. Indeed, it had become a tear which under the force of the gale was creeping sideways across his face.

My heart sank. No doubt he was used to this kind of show – there were probably a hundred impudent young pups with fine words at the ready scrambling across the mountains at this very moment, all eager to be taken on as his next pupil. My only course was to prove to him that my reputation was no lie: I sprang up and took my bow off my shoulder. As I was tautening the drawstring, I glanced at him. His head tilted forward a fraction. I drew an arrow, and addressed the distant target.

This was a daunting sight. The target was at the most distant extremity of the range, and there was also the question of the wind, which keened and swiped, tormenting any loose vegetation as a callous predator tosses the helpless body of his prey. Under such conditions an accurate shot was all but impossible. Nevertheless, my entire cause rested upon my succeeding, and my pride rose up. Why should I complain that the wind was behaving as it always had done, and always would? Was I, in spite of my boasts, fit only to shoot arrows in the still places, in the calm, warm folds of the earth far below where mundane humanity dozed in a fluffy heap like so many thousand dormice? I had in my hands the finest weapon made by Man, who thrived and overcame Nature in every corner of the world. As I was the finest archer, I too would prevail in this place through the calm application of my superior powers.

    I peered intently towards the target, seeing the outcrops of rock to each side and noting how the passage of the wind was affected as it rampaged around the plateau. And then I noted this again, to see how not one but many currents were swooping and competing for possession of the land. I crouched and watched, becoming a still, silent figure, caring nothing for the stinging slap of the wind in my face. All has its pattern, and I could ascertain by marking the circulating clouds how the winds increased and decreased in ferocity as the storm moved, presenting first its shoulder and then the protected heart before the other, equally unforgiving arm came swinging round to swipe at us with its shivering flail.

    As Yun-Pi waited, waiting in his wisdom and knowledge for the one who could not only talk but meet the challenge, I made all the necessary observations and calculations, until the howling chaos of this wild place was as orderly and predictable to me as a formal dance in a garden court. Finally I stood straight up, and to demonstrate my defiant intent I threw off my cape, predicting without an error the gust of wind that would fold it and carry it to a nearby rock. I glanced at Yun-Pi to see if this little gesture had been noted, and thought I saw the ghost of a smile cross his face.

    Once more relegated down among fools, I fixed my eye on the target and took aim. The very centre of it was a pale yellow lozenge, no bigger than a pinprick to me, but I looked hard until it became a blinding point of light. There was nothing in the whole universe but that instance, nothing but darkness. I loosed. The arrow pierced the adversarial wind, growling low as it sprang. It was true. It was the finest, the greatest arrow I had ever shot; it conquered the storm, defied the limits of human skill, and flew straight to the heart of the target.

I yelled in triumph, and had picked up a flat stone and shied it across the plateau floor before realising that as yet Yun Pi would reveal nothing to me. His look, however, told me a great deal about what I had already learned and still more about what I was to discover; and that as yet I was not ready for these lessons, and could only know disappointment that my brilliant shot had earned me no praise.

There was nothing for it but to perform my feat again, to convince him that the first had been no fluke. I took up my bow once more, balanced the arrow and drew back the string, my furious gaze unaware of anything but the tiny, distant spot of my goal.

The weather was always changing, and the storm was building in force. Nonetheless, this was all within my observations, and as I felt the wind tug at my clothes I recalculated and checked the intended trajectory of the arrow. But now the target, the rocks that marked the distances and the wind-directing outcrops to either side were overtaken in my sight by a billowing darkness that was not part of the weather, but some part of my mind, an obstruction in my own concentration that prevented me from fixing the target with an unmissable line of sight.

Although my arms were beginning to ache with the effort of keeping the bow drawn, I remained calm. Maintaining concentration is no easy task; to achieve the clear, certain fix on the target was a matter not only of resolving every material uncertainty in the arrow's flight but also of keeping at bay the manifold other concerns of life, starting with my physical discomfort and the intense cold. And now, descending into the labyrinth of my conscious knowledge, I realised that my great desire to be champion was thundering so loudly it destroyed my ability to concentrate on the task in hand. I attacked this beast with a prayer for humility and applied my devotion to the high goal of transcendent perfection, against which my own life stood surety.

This however was not enough to banish the black storm in my vision. I was instead beset with misgivings as to the course that had brought me here. For the first time in many months I thought of my father and mother, how they had wept when I set out, certain that I would be killed at some moment in my impetuous quest. And what of my own teacher at home, to whom I owed ten thousand hours of patient care and correction, whose glory it was that I had come to exhibit such talent? And the others to whom I owed so much more than passing thanks - the friends and lovers who had unstintingly accommodated my private boasts, my true pomp, the voice of my own swollen pride?

My arms were screaming out now, but I ground my teeth together and drove through the storm in my head. Tears coursed down my face as I mentally held close to me all the people whom I had for so long held at bay, kissing them, thanking them, stumbling over unfamiliar words of love and gratitude. The burning pain along my shoulders and forearms I accepted as some token of my atonement for the pain I had caused. At last my vision began to clear. The swaying, blurred shadows sank down into the familiar cracks and crags of the rocks and the last tails of the furious, black-edged maelstrom spiralled into the distance, revealing to me, shining, the lustrous gemstone of the target, which now seemed almost close enough to pluck. I loosed. Before the arrow had even moved I knew it was good. The abrupt whine of the shaft startled me, sensible as I was in the soft tears of my remorse. But it was a shot every bit as good as the first: now two sets of feathers clustered together in the target, and not a breath could go between the two arrows.

Feeling like a man who has carried a heavy burden for a thousand miles, I turned heavily towards Yun-Pi. "There's your proof." I told him, flatly. "There is no better shooting of arrows in this world. Who is the man who can outdo me?" Do not think I was disrespectful. The lack of reverence in my address was not due to arrogance, but because I was speaking now from the knowledge in my heart that I had learned the lesson for which I had come here. My flatness of tone was not the grudging voice of the fledgling who resents his guardian; it was a mere statement of fact, suspended in the air, placed simply before him in the cathedral of understanding that had grown up between us.

But he had not done with me yet. There remained one arrow in my quiver. I drew it out and looked hard at the close-veined wood as if it held the answer to the questions he forced me to ask. I found my next words in that moment of contemplation. "This last arrow of mine will be a contest" I said to him. "I shall fire, and then I shall stand where you stand to see if you can do as well as me, for I am as sure that I am the archer for whom you have been waiting on this barren plain for all these years. I am the one. If you beat me, you may kill me, for I have dealt you an extraordinary insult. But if I win, as I think I may, then I will kill you, and go down from this place to tell everyone of my victory, as is the custom in my part of the world."

Still he said nothing, but his head remained bowed, as if he were intent on the stony ground. I waited in vain for some hint that we had reached the end of the game. There was more yet to come. I was in no doubt that he would, if the contest went to him, take me up on the offer of my life. I bowed in return, turned and took aim. The bright star of the target's centre gleamed an instant and died as I knew it would. I groaned in the darkness and bore the redoubled agony of the prolonged stretching of the bowstring as the enormity of my words scourged my mind. They overwhelmed me. Black, icy waves of confusion came crashing down on me, wrecking my concentration. My arms were like a red-hot iron band tightening around my shoulders; in the centre of my chest my heart prepared to give up the struggle. I could see no target, no rocks, no plateau, nothing. Only the occasional glint of a sapphire-blue blade of grass, sometimes below me in the maelstrom, sometimes above my head. I must have been writhing and staggering. I cried out:

"Yun-Pi! My teacher! Please, I beg you! I am blind! Am I facing the target? Silence from Yun Pi: only the ecstatic scream of the storm.

"Yun-Pi! I cannot feel my hands in the cold! Is my finger drawn level with my lip?"

Darkness, howling, madness, despair. I no longer knew, no longer hoped for anything, even the ceasing of the pain. I could no longer feel the bow or the string, or the arrow.

"Yun-Pi! Is...is the arrow gone?"

Out of the darkness came a cold fist, smashing into my head. I yelled, and struggled, to find that I had struck my head against the ground in falling. My blood was on the rocks. I dragged myself to my feet. One eye was closing due to the bruise, so I could not be sure by looking down the range what had happened to my arrow. I staggered towards the target. It was a very long way; I could hardly drag my tired body along. Finally I got there, to see my three arrows clustered together in the tiny yellow heart of the target, and if it were not for the thickness of the arrows themselves they would all have been in its absolute centre.

I leaned against the target and heaved the arrows out, then, gripping them in the frozen claw of one hand, I set out back to the tiny black figure of Yun-Pi. The weather was getting worse. The storm seemed to be trapped up here on the plateau with us, but she did not appear interested in anything that took place on the archery range: she continued to rail at some unknown yet greater enemy, rushing across the plain to one possible exit only to rise up at the very edge and turn back with a howl, forever fleeing, forever castigating those who fell in her path. And as I staggered to a halt where my own blood had frozen on the rock where I had fallen, I felt myself slowing, my arms stiffening, unable to let fall the arrows as ice gathered in my exhausted veins. My face became an inexpressive mask.

"Yun-Pi!" I murmured, quietly and coldly. "Here is my bow, and here are my arrows. Use them if you will, or use your own. The choice is yours. But I will see you fire an arrow before I address you again. If you do not answer my challenge, you are dead to me!"

He did not raise his head. The wind thrashed his shoulders. I felt a terrible fear, worse than any I had known, but I forced myself to stand up to him.

"Yun-Pi!" I shouted at his tiny head, but my own voice sounded distant and broken, like the involuntary caw of a bird that is dying in flight, its brain unable to tell the air's resistance from its own unresponsive wings. "You have watched me this afternoon: you cannot doubt my dedication, my mental strength, and my skill. Yes, I have learned more from you today than in all the years I trained at home. But I have learned it in one afternoon! There is no swifter student than I! And it is impossible to shoot any better than I have done! Before you stands the inheritor of your fame. There is no archer greater than I now living." I was whispering, doubting my voice could even be heard now. "So, admit it - or prove me a fool!"

A tremendous gust came charging across the plateau and Yun-Pi fell forward on his face, his hands still clasped before his navel. His head hit the ground with a crack, and he did not move. Nor did his legs bend, frozen as they were. With the fading vision of my one remaining eye I saw extending from the black cloth on his back the old, wind-worn remnant of an arrow of a type completely unknown to me.

—ooOoo—

Peter Burgess is an artist working in various media. **The Archer** *is a story from a collection-in-progress.*

THE QUARRY

Helen Derry

Brambles tore Alfie's cheeks and nettles stung his ankles as he ran mindlessly, like a rabbit caught in the headlights of a car, through the dense wood. His breathing was ragged as he struggled to fill his lungs, the pain in his chest unbearable. He drove himself until his legs collapsed under him and he fell, gashing his knee and jarring his wrist.

Alfie pushed himself upright and leant against the corrugated bark of an old tree, trying to gather his thoughts which had scattered in his panic. All he could see was Steve's white face and imploring eyes. All he could hear was the boy's terrified scream which faded as he dropped out of sight.

That morning, the last of the summer holidays, had been full of promise. Alfie had drawn his curtains on a perfect blue sky with scudding clouds. He had thrown on his torn jeans and a paint-stained T-shirt, run his fingers through his dark curly hair, grabbed the hammer that his grandmother had given him for his twelfth birthday and raced downstairs for breakfast.

His mother was feeding baby Charlotte, who looked disgusting with Weetabix smeared all over her small face. Steve was playing on his Nintendo and ignored Alfie.

'Hi, Mum. Can I have some sandwiches? Egg and mayonnaise, please. And an apple and juice. I'll do them if you're busy with Lotty.'

Alfie hated making sandwiches but didn't want to risk a refusal. His mother was always pre-occupied nowadays. He longed for that time before he was ten when it had been just the two of them. But Steve's dad, David, had come along and that was that. No more trips to the Geology Museum, no more holidays scrambling along the beach at Lyme Regis hunting for fossils and no more evenings on the settee with a curry takeaway and the latest Harry Potter.

'Course you can, darling. Boil the eggs for ten minutes. Mayonnaise in the fridge. Where are you off to?'

'Dane's Quarry. I went to the library on Saturday and they had an exhibition. There was this ginormous ammonite discovered by a schoolmaster, George Tait, in 1890. No details about where it was found but I discovered that limestone was first dug from the quarry in 1888. Seems too good to be a coincidence.'

'Quite the detective!' she laughed.

It was like old times chatting to his mum and having her full attention. But suddenly it was all spoiled.

'Take Steve with you. I'm sure he'd be fascinated.'
Steve looked up.

'Fascinated with what, Mum?'

Alfie hated that word. She wasn't Steve's mum. He didn't call David "dad". Why would he? He'd got a dad, even though he wasn't around much. But that wasn't the point, was it?

'Fossils in Dane's Quarry. You'd enjoy that. Tell Alfie what sort of sandwiches you'd like.'

'I'm happy playing with my Nintendo, Mum. Besides, I planned to take some photos for the school competition.'

'Go and take photos of the fossils. No one else will have done that'

Alfie knew she was just trying to palm him off with Steve so she could have a bit of peace.

'Mum, I want to go by myself. I can concentrate better. I'm sure Steve would rather take photos alone.'

Steve grinned slyly and Alfie knew he was going to come to the quarry just out of spite.

'No. I'd love to go with Alfie. Fossils make great shapes. I'll go and put some old clothes on and get my camera. Oh, and cheese and pickle sandwiches please, Alfie.'

They had walked in heavy silence to Dane's Quarry, three miles or so along a narrow path through dense woodland. Alfie was determined not to speak first and so was his stepbrother. Suddenly a roebuck bounded across their path, wild- eyed and glossy-coated. They exclaimed with delight and Steve fumbled for his camera, snapping its rump as it flicked its heels and vanished as fast as it had come. They laughed together at the photo.
'I won't take the world by storm with that!' said Steve. After that they chatted like normal twelve year olds about school, football and the latest computer games until they reached Dane's Quarry. Alfie had stuffed his pocket geology book into his rucksack along with his hammer and sandwiches. They sat on a large rock side by side and ate half their sandwiches while he showed Steve pictures of trilobites and ammonites and told him about the various geological ages and the inland seas that had covered the area. Steve's eyes glazed over when Alfie got excited about the formation of the earth.
'God, Alfie. I can see how dinosaurs and early cavemen can be fascinating, but all this dry as dust stuff before living creatures is mind-blowingly boring.'
'Then why did you come, you moron? I didn't want you. Mum forced me to bring you and now you're going to ruin my day.'
He stuffed his sandwiches back in with the book and stomped off towards the edge of the quarry to examine rocks with his pocket magnifying glass. Steve took a few photos of the clouds, the trees and the bracken and then lost interest. He lolled around on the rock whistling tunelessly and then curiosity got the better of him and he started turning over stones and examining rocks.

Alfie saw what he was doing out of the corner of his eye but chose to ignore him. He found various parts of trilobites but no perfect specimens. He caressed the samples, enjoying the coil of the spirals. Then he spotted the wider curve of an ammonite beneath a frond of bracken. He dropped into a crouch and examined it more carefully. Only a quarter of the shell was visible so he picked the stone up and brushed the loose soil away. He chipped gently with the sharp end of his hammer at the surrounding stone, millimetre by millimetre. The shell gradually emerged like a butterfly from a chrysalis.

'Wow! What've you got there?'

Steve's sudden appearance broke Alfie's concentration and the hammer slipped and the ammonite snapped in two. Alfie lost his cool and shouted, 'Now look what you've made me do, you idiot! That was a perfect specimen and now it's ruined.'

'I'm really sorry, Alfie. I was just curious, that's all. I wanted to see what you'd got.'

Alfie threw the two halves hard at Steve's feet but immediately felt ashamed of his temper. He was really upset at the loss of such a fine ammonite but knew in his heart that Steve had only been showing an interest. Embarrassed, he turned his back on his step- brother and continued quartering the rock pavement above the quarry.

Steve, his red hair stiff with sweat and his freckled skin pink with sunburn and shame, nearly followed him to apologise again but instead decided to make amends by finding a replacement for the damaged fossil. In his distraction he did not notice that his search had taken him towards the edge of the quarry until, head throbbing with the late afternoon heat and sweat trickling into his eyes, he was just about to give up when he saw a giant snail-like shape etched into a rock half a metre below him. He shouted with excitement and Alfie, despite himself, rushed over to see what Steve had found. Steve was lying on a slab of rock above the ammonite, reaching with outstretched arms towards the fossil.

'Don't, Steve. Don't! It's too far.'

But Steve shook his head stubbornly, determined to make amends to his brother. His fingers made contact with the rock and he smiled triumphantly.

'Hold my legs, Alfie. I can reach it. I can.'

Alfie lay down and grabbed Steve's ankles. Steve, feeling secure, made one last lunge for the ammonite but the pebbles beneath him glided over the limestone and his body slid in slow motion towards the edge of the quarry. He twisted backwards grasping desperately for a handful of grass or bracken but his fingers clutched at thin air. Alfie hung on to his ankles but found himself dragged forward.

'Help me!' screamed Steve's mouth and his pleading eyes urged Alfie to cling on; but finally a shameful self-preservation instinct kicked in and Alfie let go just as he was about to follow Steve into the void. He watched the body bounce off the rock face and land far below in dense bushes. He lay panting and staring down at his brother's Manchester United T-shirt willing him to move; but the body was motionless. He heard rough sobs and looked round but realised they were his.

'Steve, I'm sorry. I let you go. I let you go.' He stood up unsteadily and then dropped to his knees retching. Standing up again, he searched frantically for a path into the quarry but the sides were sheer. He threw down his precious hammer and leaving his rucksack ran blindly.

Alfie dug out a grubby hanky from his pocket and tied it round his gashed knee; but within seconds it was stained scarlet with his blood. He reached behind and grasped the rough bark. Hauling himself slowly upwards he stood breathing heavily, wincing at the pain in his wrist. He had to get help. Steve just had to be alive. Alfie took an unsteady step and then tottered into a run again. Dusk was falling and he lost the path repeatedly.

Suddenly he stumbled onto a tarmacked road and he knew he was nearly home. Staggering with exhaustion he turned into his driveway and shouted for his mother. She threw open the door, face white with anxiety and flung her arms around him.

'Where were you, Alfie? I was worried sick. I thought you'd had an accident. Where's Steve?'

He hung his head, refusing to look her in the eye.

'Where's Steve? David's been out looking for you both.'

'It's my fault. It's all my fault, Mum. I didn't want him to come and now he's dead and I'll never see him again."

His legs collapsed and she caught him before he hit the path. Half carrying and half dragging him into the house, she laid him on the sofa and coaxed the garbled story out of him. She phoned the police just as David came in after his fruitless search.

Alfie buried his head in the cushions to avoid looking at Steve's father. But all he could see in the darkness were his brother's pleading eyes.

They wouldn't take him to look for Steve's body. The police doctor who accompanied the search party declared him to be suffering from shock and exhaustion. He lay in the bedroom he shared with Steve, staring at the empty bed, grasping the skinny ankles again and reliving the last moments before the plunge into nothingness. And then he was Steve spinning through space screaming. He felt the hard rock rushing up to meet him and covered his face before the impact.

He woke to hear voices below. He crept out, desperate to know the worst but unwilling to give up the faint hope that lurked unreasonably within him. He crouched on the landing peering through the banisters. Gruff voices mingled with his mother's light voice. He could only pick out a few words.

'Amazing luck … bushes broke his fall … nearly seventy feet. Foot or two either side … big rocks … smashed skull.'
Alfie broke cover and rushed downstairs into his mother's arms.

'There, there, Alfie. Steve's going to be alright. He suffered concussion, a dislocated collarbone and a broken leg.

David's with him now at the hospital. But he asked for you. Says you tried to save him. And he wants to go back with you for the ammonite, darling.'

'No way. It can stay where it is. I nearly lost my brother because of the stupid thing. It's been there for a few million years and it'll be there a million years from now if I have anything to do with it.'

THE VICTIM

Helen Derry

The forefinger, peat-brown, skin wrinkled like ancient leather stretched over the bones beneath, beckoned from the sour earth.

'Ben, come here. Quick!'

Ben rose from the shards of pottery he was photographing and crouched next to her, his long legs doubled up awkwardly. She turned and smiled at her lover.

'What've you got, Maria?'

'Don't know yet, but it looks promising.'

With her pointed trowel, she teased the soil from beneath the finger, using a brush to clear the loose earth. The other fingers, curled like a hawk's talons, appeared and finally the thumb, broken at an impossible angle. They looked at each other and Ben went to fetch his own trowel. Maria sipped cold water from her flask, waiting and thinking.

Under a leaden grey winter's sky, together they worked their way downwards. The knuckles strained against the fleshless skin and there were sunken hollows between the tendons. Finally they reached the wrist. Maria flinched and drew in a sharp breath. She dropped the trowel. Ben turned in surprise. She was never clumsy. He was startled: her nostrils were flared, her eyes dilated, and her lips bloodless, stretched tight in distress. He put a protective arm round her shoulders.

'It's OK, my love. Don't worry.' He laughed nervously. Maria remained frozen. He followed her gaze and saw the deep line round the wrist. He took her brush and with skilled fingers cleaned the soil away. A leather thong had cut into the discoloured skin. At first he thought it was one of the decorative bracelets worn by Saxon warriors in battle; but it led to another wrist and the cord was knotted, binding the hands together.

They worked hard until they had exposed the second hand. The perfectly preserved nails dented the skin of the palm. The hands met as in prayer. They knelt and stared. A tear rolled down Maria's cheek. She closed her eyes and the smell of death was in her nostrils.

She was a girl again, kneeling at the rim of a pit, the searing hot sun beating down on her bare head. Beautiful mountains surrounded the valley of Vukovar but Maria only had eyes for the floor of the pit and ears for the rhythmic swing and thud of the shovels wielded by old men and boys as they dug away the infill. Black clad women and children held each other's hands in silence, united in dread, fingering their rosaries. Suddenly, there was a gasp as old Matthias, sweat streaming down his wrinkled forehead into his ragged white beard, dropped his shovel and fell to his knees scrabbling at the dirt with his cracked fingernails. The other men and boys crowded round, blocking the women's view. Then they crossed themselves and, dropping to their knees, bowed their heads.

The women moaned and Maria stood up to catch a glimpse of a sight that was burned on her memory forever: two hands reaching towards the sky, bound tightly together. 200 bodies were exhumed from that mass grave: civilians, prisoners of war, women, and a boy of sixteen, her brother Marc. They had been torn from their hospital beds by enemy soldiers and, after being tortured, were murdered at the edge of the pit they had been forced to dig, and then flung in like so many dead animals.

She felt Ben's arms around her and he was stroking her cheek like a horse whisperer gentling a terrified mare.

'Maria, talk to me. What on earth's wrong, darling?'

Weeping, she told him how the bound hands had brought back the full horror of her brother's murder in Croatia. The war crimes tribunals had helped but the death sentences could never wipe away Marc's cruel death. Maria couldn't wait to get away from Croatia and even her poor parents, to leave all that misery and mourning behind.

'As soon as I was old enough I came to England... to study and to work. The rest you already know.'

After a brilliant academic career, Maria had made her mark as an archaeologist which was why Ben had hired her as his deputy for this dig at Holy Well. But, despite all her success, Ben knew now that Maria had not moved on. She was still grieving. He pulled her gently to her feet.

'Come on then. It's getting dark and you're shivering. Anyway, we've got to report this find to the coroner before we can proceed.'

That evening in the B and B they were staying in, switched on her laptop and researched the finding of mummified bodies all over the world: Tollund man in Denmark, Lindow man in England, the Inca ice-maiden sacrificed on a high Andean peak. She studied the photographs of the dark brown, flattened, barely human corpses with their hooded eyes and evidence of their cruel deaths: the rope round the neck, the axe-shaped hole in the head, sometimes even the head severed.

Most of these bodies were from the Iron Age. Holy Well, at the foot of Sugar Loaf Hill, together with Caesar's Camp, made up the site of a small village around 1800 BC. Later, it was a watering hole where pilgrims stopped to drink on their way to Canterbury. However, Maria and Ben were excavating a possible Saxon site.

A week later, the coroner gave the go-ahead and Ben and Maria proceeded with the excavation. The body was lying face down in a foetal position and they could see no signs of a violent death. The back of the skull, with its thick hair stained an orange-red by the bog, was intact; no garrote or noose encircled the neck. There were no stab wounds from weapons. Maria began to wonder whether the young man had been bound and buried alive. She shuddered. She had always dreaded that Marc had still been breathing when his murderers had heaped soil upon him.

Ben scraped the earth from the face and she saw the eyes pressed tight shut and the young face now as wizened as an old man. And then the gaping neck and dark-stained soil surrounding it. His throat had been slit. She leant forward to study a rust coloured area in the ground below his neck. She picked at it carefully with her trowel and a shape emerged: a cross!

'He was a Christian, Ben. This can't be an Iron Age body. Whoever killed him didn't bother to steal the cross because it wasn't gold or silver. Do you think he was a prisoner or a hostage? Or a sacrifice? He can't have been a warrior killed in battle with his hands tied behind his back.'

'Too early to tell. But it's certain the poor sod was murdered by someone or other, whatever the motive. The coroner wants some samples sent off for radio carbon dating before we move the body. Then an autopsy will give us a lot more information.'

'And a DNA sample to help us establish his racial origins.'

The radio carbon printout from the lab., two weeks later, pointed to the 9th Century, probably the latter half. The DNA sample taken from the body confirmed a Saxon or Viking origin. Their guess that their victim was about 15 to 18 was confirmed by bone and tooth samples.

Maria consulted her well-thumbed Anglo-Saxon Chronicle to check the movements of the Vikings in Kent before and during the reign of Alfred, King of Wessex, who repelled the heathens with great difficulty. She found an entry for 865 AD that caught her eye:

'Her sæt se hæthene here on Tenet ond genam frith with Cantwarum'

The Viking army remained in Thanet and made peace with the Kentishmen who promised them money to leave them alone. Under cover of the amnesty the heathen army stole away by night and ravaged eastern Kent.

Maria imagined the boy left with the old men to guard the women and children by the warriors who had gone to the peace talks. Torches suddenly blazing out of the moonless night setting roofs alight, guttural foreign voices and the terror of capture. He would have tried to fight like his chieftain father but they had laughed and picked him up like a puppy. They tied his hands and forced him to watch his mother and sisters being raped before slitting his throat as if he were a pig and throwing him into a boggy area by the spring. Seeing his cross, they joked that his God had allowed Christ to be murdered too.

Much later she stood by the glass case in the British Museum watching her Saxon. How vulnerable he looked, curled up naked, on his side, hands pinioned, his young flesh fallen away and his fair skin and hair stained by the acid of the bog, exposed to the gaping crowds. She had dragged him from the earth in the name of science. Her brother had at least had a Christian burial, mourned by his family and the remaining villagers.

It was time to celebrate Marc's young life with her parents.

She turned to Ben.

'Let's go to Croatia this Easter. I want to introduce you to my family.'

—ooOoo—

Helen Derry was an English teacher for 28 years. She retrained as a lawyer and practised family law for 10 years. She is married and has three children and eight grandchildren. She enjoys watercolour painting, bridge, sailing, high mountain walking, and travelling all over the world. She started writing when she retired, mainly short stories but is also eight chapters into a novel.

AN EDUCATION

Grant Gibson

I had spent the first year or so of my secondary schooling at an excellent, boys grammar school in Folkestone, but sadly, for me it was not a happy experience. In four terms I had slipped from the B stream to C and was heading remorselessly for D. My parents, both teachers, decided that a different approach was called for.

So they sent me to Cranbrook, a traditional, all boys, minor public school, nestling in the heart of the very beautiful Weald of Kent, as a boarder. The school is no longer minor, in fact, it is one of the best in the country but in those days pupil acceptance was based more on your sporting, acting or shooting ability than academic prowess. As a consequence, I sailed through the interview process and was accepted.

It was the spring of 1966 and the school was soon to celebrate its fourth centenary, having been established by royal charter in Elizabethan times. The architecture of its main educational buildings was classical and imposing, while its boarding houses, scattered all over the local town, were a mixture of the suburban and utilitarian. The school's ethos was very much to turn out a pupil who was fully rounded in all aspects of life, including the arts and sport, particularly the latter. Academic endeavour and achievement, whilst recognised as being important, was not the be all and end all. This was my kind of school!

The headmaster, John Kendall Carpenter, had been England's rugby captain in the early fifties and was later to be President of the England Rugby Union, in which capacity he acted as one of the key founders of the Rugby World Cup. So rugby, or 'rugger' as we called it then, was inevitably a major focus for the school, if not its primary one.

Its traditions and customs had not changed much for many decades; we still wore boaters, white shirts with detached stiff collars and studs, and absolutely no elastic sided shoes! Fags still featured (just), as did beatings by staff and prefects, with cane or shoe and a beating from the headmaster was, not surprisingly, something to be dreaded.

Equally, the teaching methods of some of their educational staff, many of whom had been at Cranbrook since before the Second World War, were set in aspic. The predilections of one or two of these masters were, to say the least, disturbing, but this was a time when speaking out was not encouraged. A good example of this was when the newly appointed chemistry master had me clearing out his predecessor's preparation room, only to discover that the majority of the specimen bottles contained some very drinkable clear spirits. The dozens of empty bottles of gin and vodka stashed away in the store cupboards just underlined the problem. It certainly helped us to understand the origin of our departing master's nickname, "Teed" (as in stewed!).

Our uniform, sports gear, trunk and tuck box were all purchased at Gorringes in Bayswater, London, and were supplemented by the school shop. In addition to the tuck box we had our own tuck shop, both of which were supposed to keep at bay our constant hunger. They didn't!

The general living conditions would be considered Dickensian today, as evidenced by unheated dormitories, where glasses of water would freeze overnight on the bedside cupboard. Baths were taken once a week and shirts changed every 2 days, although collars were issued daily.

The dining hall was presided over by Dick, the butler. His persona was of a shabby pre-war movie matinee idol crossed with an English bulldog. Heavily Brylcreemed thinning hair and a greying pencil moustache complemented his bulging white jacket complete with black tie, neither of which was particularly clean. I recall that his voice had the gruffness and volume of a regimental sergeant major. He certainly commanded attention.

Dick had one major problem; he did not like boys and, what's more, he clearly disliked supervising the feeding of them, which was a slight problem, given his job! The zeal that he brought to this slightly warped interpretation of his role, i.e. the protection of all things edible, was akin to that of a prison guard. He was utterly ruthless and wielded his bread knife in such a menacing manner that only a fool would attempt to sneak an extra sandwich from under his nose.

The boys themselves were responsible for dining table serving duties, either on a roster or punishment basis. The common parlance for this activity was "Swab" and, at meal times, regular calls for a "Swab" were to be heard at table, as was the schoolboy lingo for different food types; slabs, grease, grit, blood sauce and the infamous "dragon's bollocks", which were, respectively, bread, margarine, sugar, tomato sauce and tinned tomatoes.

The food was not only appalling but also, even without Dick, insufficient. It was no coincidence that obesity simply did not exist; we were constantly starving. As a consequence, our pocket money of two pounds for the entire term was almost totally spent on food – but it was never sufficient.

At just twelve years old and driven by hunger, I turned to crime; sorry, I should have said private enterprise.

1. Private enterprise

Ginger beer seemed to me to be a great way of making money and so became my means to an end, the end here being food. If you have ever made homemade ginger beer you will know that you start with a ginger beer "plant". This simply consists of a jam jar, some ginger powder, yeast and water. You daily add yeast and ginger and, after a couple of weeks, you use this as a base concentrate for your ginger beer drink.

Now, what is interesting is that each time you make a batch of ginger beer you divide your "plant" in two. Thus, in another two weeks time, you are able to make double the amount of ginger beer that you had made previously, and so on; in other words compound growth. It was to be my first lesson in economics and it was painful.

I had established my market with fellow twelve-year-old members of the junior dorm. The freshly made ginger beer went down a treat; my resultant financial reward enabled me to eat to my heart's content (well almost). All was well. Initially, demand outstripped supply, but after a few weeks, the compound growth effect meant that I needed to find a store facility for my unsold stock. I found this at the back of the drying room, which housed the boys' laundered sports clothes, sheets and towels. The storage arrangements had been made with the blessing of Matron and the housemaster, who felt that I was to be encouraged for showing such positive initiative. They were soon to be very disillusioned.

Laundry rooms are by definition warm places, and this one was all the more so, since it also housed the boiler; this and the fact that my education thus far had not embraced fermentation, proved disastrous. In all innocence, ignorance you may say, I had not only given a turbo charge to the fermentation process but by building up a stock and not giving much attention to date rotation, I had allowed the alcoholic content to rocket. To be fair though, I simply had no idea that Gibson's Patent Ginger Beer would prove to be alcoholic at all.

It all started innocuously enough, manifesting itself in the strange behaviour of certain of the very young boarders. My over-supply had got to the stage where I needed to expand my market and so I had targeted the first year dormitory who were between ten and eleven years old. They absolutely loved the stuff but their erratic behaviour did begin to cause concern. Initially, it was just laughed off, as when a certain ten year old told his dormitory prefect how much he fancied his mother, but the alarm bells really began to sound later that day, when another ten year old was found staggering around a playing field, cuddling a ginger beer bottle. Events were moving rapidly, as were the suspicions of many of the staff. I don't think, however, that anyone was prepared for the evening's shock.

It was during supervised prep (homework) that night, when a loud bang was heard. It sounded as though someone had fired a gun just outside the boarding house which, given the close proximity of the school's shooting range, was not an altogether ridiculous assumption. We all ran to the window to see who the culprit was;

'Sit down Gibson', said the duty prefect; I did as I was told.

The second and third bangs, which were heard a few minutes later, were more akin to explosions and by now even the prefects were alarmed.

At this point, the housemaster and Matron appeared at the door of the prep room and appeared to be somewhat agitated. I couldn't help noticing that Matron's hair looked very wet; this was strange, as it had been a beautiful summer's day with not a drop of rain to be seen.

'Gibson', shouted the housemaster, 'come here!'

I did as I was told but, as I approached them, I took on board that it was not just Matron's hair that was wet, so too were her clothes…hmmm. As I followed them out of the room, I felt, for the first time, a tingling feeling in the back of my neck. It was not to be the last time I experienced that sensation!

The housemaster demanded to know how many bottles of ginger beer there were stored in the drying room.

'Oh, I am not sure,' said I, 'probably about sixty'.

The housemaster started speaking to me in what sounded like a very strained voice, which raised a pitch when we heard another loud bang.

Evidently Matron had been hanging clothes in the drying room when two of my ginger beer bottles had self-combusted. One bottle had simply pushed the cork out and spewed ginger beer everywhere including onto her clothing, and the other had literally exploded, shedding glass and contents all over the room. It was the latter explosion, which had driven Matron from the boiler room, in a very distressed state, to seek out the housemaster. Seemingly, I had not been too careful in my selection of glass bottles and this was proving to be a negligent act of some proportion.

As Matron had taken the brunt of these explosions she was clearly not too impressed with me but the housemaster was on an altogether different plane of anger. By now word had reached him regarding the drunken behaviour of the under-elevens in his charge, which would have been bad enough, but having to deal with what was rapidly becoming a major incident was far from pleasing him. In terms of danger, ginger-beer-drenched towels, sheets and clothing was one thing, but shards of exploding glass was quite another. Another explosion was heard.

It was decided, for reasons of health and safety (at least I think that was what they said), to switch the boiler off and seal the room for the night. The thinking of the housemaster was that by the morning things would have settled down and an incursion could then be attempted.

The next few hours were difficult, punctuated as they were by loud bangs and the odd rant by the housemaster. Of course, for small boys this was the cause of absolute hilarity and delight, but inevitably, it encouraged indiscipline. As a result, the prefects, who ran things at night, were also pretty fed up with me.

It was all very difficult for yours truly. As far as I could see, I had gone from 'admirable chap' to 'pariah' in the time it took to pop a cork (so to speak). Not only that, Gibson's Patent Ginger Beer Emporium was closed, and without any compensation. Life was so unfair.

2. Sport

Before Cranbrook, my previous sporting life had been limited. Although I enjoyed watching football (soccer) I could not play it very well and as that was the main sport of the grammar school that I previously attended, I had had little engagement with games. That all changed at Cranbrook.

I was brutally introduced to a very different world of strange games and their associated components; fives, rackets, squash, hockey, boxing and rugger, to mention a few. I say brutally, as my first exercise in the gymnasium ended in my hospitalisation.

Initiation ceremonies were part and parcel of a new boy's life and this particular initiation certainly had impact. A few of the older boys thought it would be excellent fun to see what a naïve new boy from the state system would do with a medicine ball. For those of you who are not aware, a medicine ball is a weighted leather ball, used mainly in training to develop abdominal muscles. They can weigh up to 12 kilos.

Now, I didn't know any of this and so, when they threw the ball at me, I kicked it back...or tried to! Even wearing my pumps (gym shoes in those days), I felt the most excruciating pain in my right big toe and fell over. I was taken up to Matron in the sanatorium who, on taking one look at the swelling appendage, called the doctor. The doctor quickly diagnosed a breakage and I was dispatched to Tunbridge Wells for the accident and emergency (A & E) hospital. I hopped into the A & E unit and three hours later I limped out with a large plaster cap on my big toe and a crutch in my hand.

Although I had been told that I would have to keep the cap on for about four weeks and that during that time I was not to put any weight on my foot, boredom and the impatience of a twelve year old, soon got the better of me. I returned, prematurely, to the scene of my injury; the gym.

This time I steered clear of the medicine ball and joined in with a five-a-side soccer game, albeit wearing an extremely large pump shoe on my right foot. Due to my restricted mobility, I was put in goal.

All went well until I over-reached myself and took a swing at the ball with my left foot, missed and kicked the gym wall: utter agony.

Once again I was carried off to the sanatorium to seek out Matron and once again she inspected a Gibson swelling appendage, called the doctor and packed me off to Tunbridge Wells. By now the hospital staff were getting to know me! Another broken big toe was diagnosed and another plaster cap fitted. With both big toes now housed in a plaster cap, hopping was, unfortunately not an option, so a pair of crutches was considered necessary and this time I "swung" out of the A & E.

As already mentioned, rugby was the key sport at Cranbrook and, by virtue of the Headmaster's own prowess and stature in the rugby union game as an ex-captain of England, we were expected to win … and win we did. In all the teams (mainly first teams) that I played in, and at every age level, I never experienced losing. That delight was to await me when I left school and entered the world of club rugby.

My first exposure to rugby football was a revelation. Given a cursory verbal explanation about the rudiments of the game, I was passed the ball and told to run and to keep going regardless, I did just that and, miracle of miracles, it worked! With the ball safely tucked under my arm, I ploughed through everyone, headed for the distant touchline and scored, how wonderful! I had found my *"métier"*.

A little later in the session, the ball was again passed to me just at the time when the master (teacher) taking our training class decided to join in and went to tackle me, I remembered what he had told me and just kept going. Unfortunately, my knee ended up in his groin with some impact and he lay, pole-axed, on the floor. He never forgot this and thereafter always held a grudge against me but he did, nevertheless, pick me for the under 13's first team.

My rugby career had started but sadly, so too had my catalogue of rugby sporting injuries, including a future fractured skull.

Rugby was not to be my only strength: hockey, swimming, squash and athletics were rapidly added to my sports portfolio. Only cricket remained outside the reach of my all-round sporting abilities, which was probably just as well, since the one and only school cricket match that I played in saw me going for a catch, missing the ball, and ending up in the sanatorium with Matron. The cricket ball had hit my mouth and pushed some front teeth through my bottom lip.

Notwithstanding my cricketing deficiencies, the summer opened up new possibilities for me in the guise of swimming and athletics.

The school had a superb outdoor heated pool set in beautiful sylvan surroundings and consequently considerable emphasis was placed on swimming, both as a basic skill and as a sport. Having lived for many years on the coast, I was already a strong swimmer and, naturally enough, I was immediately attracted to any aquatic event. My first participation in a swimming-sports event was an internal school competition for which I had been picked to represent my 'house' in a backstroke race. The day duly arrived, and with a crowd of some two hundred boys watching, I took up my position in the second lane.

As I am sure you know, a backstroke race requires the competitors to take up a foetal position in the water, facing the rear of the pool with your back turned towards the lane that you will swim down. The start is half 'backward push-off' and half 'back flip' away from the pool wall. This is achieved by drawing your knees up to your stomach, pressing your feet firmly against the pool wall while using your hands to hold yourself 'ball like' tightly in this position with the aid of a bar. This pool had no such facility, so instead we used the pool's overhanging concrete slabs to grip until we were released backwards by the starter's gun.

Unfortunately, the starting gun did not trigger my 'release' but, rather, cement did – well, faulty cement, actually. Before the gun was fired, the slab of concrete that I'd been tensing against came away from its fixing in its entirety and landed on me very painfully. Its weight pushed me under the rapidly discolouring water caused by the discharge of blood from my badly scratched chest and stomach.

This episode had not exactly gone unnoticed. The gun had been fired but, when the start for the boys either side of me was impeded by my "incident", it was fired again to recall the competitors. The same boys helped me out of the water but I was struggling and the reason why became all too clear when I finally emerged, looking like an extra from *Jaws*. This interlude, of course, provided great hilarity for the assembled spectators – at least, once they saw that I was not mortally wounded, it did.

My conveyance on a stretcher to the sanatorium and the tender mercies of Matron was rapid – unlike my emergence from it, which did not occur for another three days!

Although a useful sprinter at 110 & 220 yards, my best athletic discipline was the discus followed (someway behind) by the javelin. I represented the school team in the discus event and house teams for both discus & javelin. Actually, it was probably just as well that it was the discus and not the javelin that became my main athletics discipline, given the inherent dangers of the javelin, which I discovered all too painfully.

Our annual athletics inter-house competition was held every May Day. This annual event was always looked forward to with great anticipation but, by the time the big day arrived it had been raining continually for over three days and puddles were scattered all over the sports field. We fully expected the fixture to be cancelled or at least postponed. Neither occurred. Instead, the decision was taken that the event should go ahead. The scene was now set for a very personally-painful day.

Traditionally, the kit that you wear when throwing the javelin is normal athletics apparel, complemented with running spikes to give you traction when throwing. Thus attired, I stepped up to take the first of my three throws. I set off, running fast down the track, trying my best to avoid the muddiest parts, and, although slipping slightly, I successfully made my first throw. My five opponents then took their turns, not without some difficulty, as each subsequent run made the track into even more of a quagmire. By the time I picked up my javelin to take my second throw, there were no longer any defining lane lines visible and rain had started to fall. I bit my lip, focused, and took off down the invisible track. As I drew the javelin back behind me, keeping my throwing arm stretched out parallel with the javelin; I reached the point of no return and went for launch, at which point disaster struck.

At the point of release, my left spiked running shoe stuck fast in the mud, causing me to stumble forward. As I fell, my right arm, which was in the process of swinging to launch the javelin, continued its arc but instead of flying through the air, it speared my right foot. I was now stuck fast in the mud.

In considerable pain, I screamed for help. The games master came to my rescue by lifting me off the ground and removing the javelin from my foot. My right running shoe had changed colour from blue to red! Two boys carried me up to the sanatorium and the tender mercies of Matron. The doctor was called and found that the end of my foot had been punctured. Stitches were applied and a tetanus injection administered. Two days in the sanatorium followed.

The competition was abandoned – health and safety, I believe!

3. Military service

I mentioned before that our school was very traditional and nowhere did this manifest itself more than in its approach to the military. The main school hall, known as "Big School", was adorned with two memorial boards listing the boys who had fallen in both the first and second world wars. It was indeed sobering. The school continued to maintain strong links with the military, and many old Cranbrookians went on to officer training at Sandhurst (Army), Cranwell (Air force) or Dartmouth (Navy).

One afternoon a week was devoted to military activities for all boys over the age of fourteen. You either joined the CCF (Combined Cadet Force – Army) or the ATC (Air Training Corps – Air force). If you were a 'conscientious objector', you could opt out and dig gardens for pensioners in the village as a member of the Social Services unit.

Liking aircraft, I decided to join the ATC. The first step was to be issued with a uniform. However, this apparently simple process proved to be a real challenge. There were two reasons for this.

The first was that of my collar size. Through playing a great deal of rugby in the scrum as a front row prop, my neck had grown to the extent that no ATC collars were available which fitted me. It's important to appreciate that the ATC shirt in those days was still a collarless garment, in the same way as that of my school uniform, so you were issued with one shirt, two collars and a tie. In my case the issue was confined to one collarless shirt, as the tie without a collar was superfluous.

The second reason was that I had a large, actually a very large, head size and my boater had been a special order. So, I was also *"sans"* an ATC beret.

My appearance on the parade ground, not surprisingly, left a great deal to be desired. I had the leather boots, I had the leather gaiters, the trousers, the brass buckled webbed belt and the jacket, but I did not have a collar, tie or hat. I looked like a cross between Alf Garnett and Rambo.

Matters were not helped by my marching abilities, or rather lack of them. My co-ordination relative to parading was, to put it mildly, dysfunctional.

Not surprisingly, I spent a lot of time sidelined, watching ATC matters from a distance. Nevertheless, the day finally came when I was actually allowed to participate in a visit to RAF Manston, where we were to take a training flight in a Chipmunk aircraft. We set off excitedly in a coach clutching our packed lunches and dressed in full uniform, except in my own case.

We were ordered not to consume our packed lunches until later when told to do so. The reason for this was never explained, but eventually became all to clear. Along with many of the other boys, I ignored this instruction.

On arriving at Manston, we were given a full briefing by the ground staff as to what we should and should not do. Of prime importance was the method of getting in and out of the cockpit and of getting on and off the aircraft wings. The Chipmunk aircraft, although very robust, was not an all-metal flying machine.in fact, its wings were mainly covered in treated fabric.

We were each issued with a parachute, which in those days was not only extremely heavy but also very cumbersome. It was strapped tightly to our backs or rather our bottoms. The idea was that, if correctly positioned in the cockpit, you would be sitting on the parachute.

Now, you need to know that my mother was only five feet tall, while my father was six foot three. I got her legs and his body. Think Toulouse-Lautrec or Max Wall and you will not be too far off. So, the way that the parachute was affixed to my body caused me to double over and made me look an awful lot like Quasimodo, hunchback and all. Although my movements were severely impaired, I was nevertheless determined to get in that aircraft; and so I joined the queue, shuffling slowly towards the aircraft runway.

It was finally my turn and I set off with some difficulty towards the taxiing Chipmunk. Somehow I managed to climb up onto the wing and tumbled clumsily into the cockpit, which contained two seats, one in front for a passenger and the other in the rear for the pilot. As we taxied out to the main runway I introduced myself to the pilot via my headphones. He seemed a friendly enough chap. The plan was to do two circuits and bumps (landings), interspersed with some acrobatics. It was the latter that I was concerned about.

We took off and went straight into a climb. Eventually, on reaching the summit of the arc, we descended upside down and proceeded to "loop the loop". This proved too much for my already consumed packed lunch, which re-emerged from my stomach in all its glory onto the roof of the cockpit and, when we straightened up, dropped onto my head and, in part, onto the pilot's head.

All banter between the pilot and myself, ceased. We did not attempt a second circuit or indeed anything else, and instead went straight in to land. I was quite shaken up and completely disoriented. This fact, when combined with the restrictive parachute that I was wearing, was a recipe for disaster.

Desperate to release myself from the dual constraints of cockpit and vomit covered uniform, I scrambled to get out as quickly as I could. Although I managed to get one leg out of the cockpit successfully, I somehow slipped with my other foot and to my horror heard the awful sound of tearing fabric. My left foot had missed the black walking strip and gone straight through the wing.

My distinguished military career came to a rapid inglorious end. I was decommissioned and sent to Social Services…

—ooOoo—

Grant Gibson was a VP of a large multinational working mainly overseas. He has since semi-retired to his home area near Hythe where he combines his time running his greeting card franchise and enjoying his grandchildren. Of late, he has started writing and recently completed his first book, an extract from which won the H G Wells Writers prize of 2011.

BLACKOUT

Tim Goss

The old man groaned. His arms ached, his legs ached and his stomach hurt. His bowels had been backed up for five days now. The Doctor had given him some potion or other to imbibe but it hadn't taken effect yet. He rubbed his hands over his naked scalp. The day nurse entered sucking a sweet.

'How are you feeling today Mr Reynolds?' she asked with a cherry-coloured smile.

Reynolds grunted. What did she expect from him? What did anyone expect from him? Rosy platitudes? He had neither the time nor the inclination for that sort of banality. Douglas Reynolds had come to realise that as death approaches, time speeds up. Like a horse returning home after a long ride, the closer it gets the speedier it trots. He had not asked to be interred in this morgue that was decided by his shit of a son.

'It's for your own good, Dad,' the boy had said as the automatic doors locked behind him. Then later, on the phone: 'The Doctors say you'll only be in there a week – two at most.' And that was four days ago.

'You haven't eaten your breakfast.' The Nurse chastised. 'You know you've got to keep your strength up.'

What the fuck for? he thought. It's not like she was about to strip off and insist he fuck her against the saline drip. Although she did have a strangely carnal spark in her blue-green eyes that beckoned him on whenever she looked at him.

'Doctor won't be happy if you don't eat,' she continued, picking up the spoon and stirring his porridge.

'I can't eat,' he growled. 'My guts feel like they're gonna explode.'

'Oh, come on, just a couple of mouthfuls. It's got honey and raisins in it.' Her eyes shone tempting him closer and closer.

Reynolds twisted his mouth into a painful smile. Nothing like dried fruit to open your bowels.

'There's a good boy,' the nurse applauded. 'You don't even have to put your teeth in for that.'

By mid-morning he had finally dislodged the remains of the porridge from his toothless gums. Food had no joy to it these days. Sucking the life out of a meal, because his dentures hurt more often than not, was by far the worst way to eat. He had tried blending foods together at home, making shakes or 'smoothies' as they now call them but it wasn't the same. He likened drinking a roast turkey meal (or mulch) through a straw to eating meat-flavoured wallpaper paste. It was thick, decidedly lumpy and made him gag more than once. The strawberry-scented shower gel his granddaughter bought him last Christmas tasted better … and it went down more easily too.

He could hear the guy in the room next door moaning. He had been moaning most of the night. The nurses were in and out of his room throughout the small hours, their rubber-soled shoes slapping against the linoleum flooring. Had he been able to sleep it would have certainly woken him. He decided to get out of bed and visit his neighbour, as no one had bothered with him for the last two hours.

The aches and pains in his legs and arms were surprisingly better for a little movement. It might even help dislodge the rotting stodge in his gut, he thought, but he wouldn't hold his breath.

Reaching the door, Reynolds knocked. No answer. He knocked again louder, still no answer. After a third attempt he decided to go in uninvited. The room was dark, the curtains drawn. The intrusive bleep, bleep, bleep of a heart monitor pierced the stuffy, stale air. The man in the bed was about his age, but he had more hair and wore a rather unruly moustache. His face was grey, reminding Reynolds of his own mortality and there was a thin crust of mucus around his nostrils. A second machine, the opposite side of the bed to the heart monitor, was rigged up to administer morphine. The man held a large red button in his grey wrinkled fingers that controlled this.

His eyes snapped opened immediately Reynolds took a step toward the bed.

'You all right?' Reynolds asked, trying not to look too deeply into the man's watery eyes.

The man groaned, his eyes becoming heavier.

'Do you want me to get you a nurse?' Reynolds continued.

Again the man groaned. Reynolds saw his thumb depress the large red button in his hand and the morphine machine hissed.

After a few seconds the man mouthed something inaudible. Reynolds moved closer to hear what he was saying.

'Not enough.' the man sighed and groaned once more.

'I'll get you a Nurse.' Reynolds said and started to back away from the bed.

The man's eyes widened. Then, in a sudden unexpected movement, he caught hold of Reynolds arm with the aid of Reynolds sleeve.

'Not enough.' he said again, straining to pull himself up

'I'll get you a nurse,' Reynolds repeated, pulling his arm away from the man's claw-like fingers, 'I'm sure they'll be able to sort you out.'

The man fell back on the bed. As his head hit the pillow he depressed the big red button once again. This time the machine remained silent.

'Not enough.' he moaned, 'not enough.'

The Nurse was severe. Reynolds heard him from his room.

'Enough is enough Mr Long. It's what the Doctor prescribed and **I** can't increase the dose.'

Just an old junky, Reynolds thought, angling for a higher dose of morphine. No doubt the man was in pain but... He'd seen it before in the hospital in West Berlin thirty years ago. That guy was a road traffic victim disabled in the accident. He was in pain too but the nurses just couldn't satisfy his craving.

Reynolds' cravings at that time were more alcoholic. He'd been admitted to the Martin-Luther-Krankenhaus, in the Schmargendorf district of Berlin, because he'd put his fist through a plate-glass window. It wasn't aimed at anyone in particular, just the frustrations of a working man abroad. He was reading Isherwood's *'Mr Norris Changes Train'* at the time and longed for the old Weimar Berlin. All he'd found though was a couple of tired drag acts and the rumour that David Bowie might be stalking the streets. Thankfully his company had footed the bill; medical costs were included in his expenses when travelling internationally. He told his boss he slipped on a rogue banana skin tossed over the wall by an angry communist.

The nurses never thanked him for alerting them to Mr. Long's craving – but what did he expect?

Reynolds' son had brought some books in for him to read. He never bothered to say hello but the Nurse who delivered them said that he sent his regards.

'I bet he did!' Reynolds scowled. To which the Nurse shuffled awkwardly, puffed up his pillows and hotfooted it out of the door. They were trained to avoid family conflicts wherever possible.

Reynolds wanted to ask how his cats were getting on without him. He had feared that the little shit wouldn't bother to feed them while he was away, so he'd asked his neighbour, Mrs. Jenkins, to pop in and make a fuss of them. She was a reliable old bird, one of the few neighbours he actually spoke to. She'd see them all right, he reassured himself. His first cat, Moses, had died young, killed by a worthless piece of human trash driving a taxicab. The bastard didn't even stop, or so he was told. Mrs. Jenkins saw the whole thing from her front garden. It was she who scooped young Moses' lifeless body off the tarmac and brought him home.

Reynolds was heart-broken. The small consolation that Moses was killed outright failed to soften the blow and he mourned for weeks. He sobbed as he buried his companion in the back garden and would cry on and off for nearly a fortnight. It was painful to look at the empty spaces where the cat slept, the empty bowls and empty bed. He missed the purring and the rubbing around his legs, the scratching at his bedroom door and the nuzzling when he was trying to read. He missed snoozing in front of the telly with the cat curled up on his legs. He had shared more with Moses than he had his own children.

It was nearly a year before he got another cat.

The first was a young stray, black with a single white spot on his chest. He'd been hanging around the garden for a couple of days, just skin and bone really, with a scraggy coat and the tip of his tail missing. Reynolds put out some food and a bowl of water and that was that. Within two days he had made himself at home.

Reynolds named him Jasper and Jasper purred whenever the old man picked him up.

The second was a great tabby queen. She carried herself like royalty, knowing she was by far the best thing in town.

Reynolds got her from the woman who owned the local Newsagent's. She mentioned to him that her mother had recently died, leaving a pile of half-finished knitting and a great tabby queen named Leila. She knew that Reynolds liked cats and was, at the time, unaware of Jasper's existence.

The old man inquired as to what would happen to Leila if no one could take her.

'Well,' the shop keeper said, fingering her hollow cheeks, 'I s'pose I'll have to have her put down.'

Reynolds agreed to take her on the spot.

The following few weeks were difficult. Jasper's suspicions of Leila ran deep and her natural arrogance only played to his feline paranoia. At one point Reynolds seriously considered re-homing her. Then he came home one afternoon and found them curled up together at the top of the stairs, purring like a couple of old diesel engines. Reynolds breathed a sigh of relief.

Once he had two cats his house and garden became a free zone for any waif or stray that was passing through the area. It was as if the word was out and the old man's property offered any feline sanctuary – a safe place to get a bowl of food and a bed for the night. Some travelling cats stayed a week, a fortnight, a month, but none stayed for good, except for Jasper and Leila.

Then two young kittens turned up, no more than six months old. Russian blues, he thought. At least, that was their colouring. Jasper and Leila took to them immediately and before long had become the kittens' surrogate parents. Reynolds named them Leaky & Lotty, more to do with the fact that the tom had a few bladder problems to begin with.

His son didn't care for cats –, another reason for the bad blood between the two. In his darker moments Reynolds could even convince himself that it was his son driving the taxicab that killed his beloved Moses. Jealousy can be a deadly emotion,

Doc Fleming did his rounds at ten in the morning. He was a traditional Doctor with half-moon glasses and red alcoholic eyes. He always knocked before entering a room but never waited to be invited in.

'So, how are you feeling today Mr…[he picked up the chart at the end of the old man's bed] … Reynolds?'

'All the better for seeing you, Doc.' Reynolds replied, smiling wryly.

'Mr Reynolds has not been eating, Doctor,' the Nurse at Fleming's side interjected. Reynolds glared at her hatefully.

'Well, that won't do,' Fleming said, peering momentarily over his glasses.

'Mmm,' he continued, 'I see you still haven't had a bowel movement,' then, turning to the Nurse, 'Tell me Nurse, has the patient been taking his medication?'

'Yes, Doctor.'

'Well, we'll increase it to four time times a day. See if that does the trick.'

Reynolds thought he saw a smile of satisfaction reflected in the nurse's otherwise emotionless features.

Fleming looked the old man in the eye. 'That should clean you out in no time,' he said, raising a knowing eyebrow.

'Any news on the results of my brain scans, Doc?' Reynolds asked, tapping his forehead with the tip of his right index finger.

'Not yet Mr…' again the patient's name eluded him, '…but I can assure you that, as soon as I know, you'll know.'

Reynolds smiled, somewhat thankfully.

It was his GP, Doctor Knowles, who informed his son that it was necessary for Reynolds to go into hospital.

She was concerned, she said, as to the frequency of the blackouts the old man had been experiencing. This suggested to Reynolds that the odd blackout was considered OK.

In the beginning he didn't really mind them too much – five or ten minutes lost from your day are hardly worth worrying about. They always occurred in the house and he never damaged himself or any of his possessions. Quiet moments, that's how he thought of them: moments of solitude and seclusion to be cherished. There had been a time many years ago, when he'd suffered from acute lapses in memory. Whole evenings lost, hours of his life never to be recovered; but he'd never passed out.

Then, about two months ago he blacked out standing in line at the Post Office. One minute he was peering into the old girl's bag that was open in front of him, the next he was being dragged up onto a plastic chair and forced to drink water from a polystyrene cup. The young woman assisting him, wearing an 'I'M

TRAINED IN FIRST AID' badge, told him he'd been out cold for nearly ten minutes. She sorted out his business, asked if there was anyone she could phone – to which the old man shook his head negatively – and sent him home in a taxi.

The next one was only a few days later. He smacked his head on the coffee table that time. When he woke up, Lotty and Leaky were curled up beside him; they had his blood on their paws and their bloody footprints marked the majestic rug in a circle round his body. Jasper was purring on the sofa watching him.

A week or so later he collapsed in the bathroom. Luckily it was only for a couple of minutes. He knew this because he was filling the bath at the time and the water had hardly risen. He dreaded to think of the mess if it had been for longer.

This continued on and off for the next few weeks.

Then he blacked out in the front garden. Mrs Jenkins found him lying in the Kerria Japonica, its bright yellow flowers hanging out of his nostrils and ears. She didn't try to move him but waited until her visitor arrived. Together they picked him up helped him into the house.

It was Mrs Jenkins who insisted he call the Doctor.

'Mr Reynolds,' she said in her best and sternest manner, 'you cannot rely on someone finding you the next time this happens. What happens if you pass out in the bath? You might drown!' She handed him the telephone. 'The Doctor will know what's best.'

Unfortunately he had to ask his son to take him into town to see the quack. The fear of collapsing en route meant that he couldn't walk, plus Reynolds refused to take a cab on the grounds that they had killed Moses, and he could not be held responsible for his actions toward any of the local drivers. Public transport was also out of the question as he'd had a nasty experience on the bus a few years ago involving a single mother, her uncontrollable brat and an umbrella.

The initial scans were taken the day he arrived. There had been another three since that time and still no news.

The constipation was a side effect, he had been told, of the medication the Doctors prescribed on admission. The medication had now been stopped but the constipation persisted.

That evening, after a particularly uneventful afternoon, Reynolds took the lift down to the garden level. He was joined in the car by two orderlies and couldn't help but overhear their conversation.
'That nurse is a peach!' stated the orderly in front of Reynolds. He kissed the tips of his index and middle finger and threw the kiss into the air with a showman's zeal.
'She was definitely looking you up and down, man,' the second said with an approving nod.
'Yeah, I'm gonna make her mine and blow her mind.' The first said with rhythmic flare and fluidity.
Reynolds coughed; he was unsure whether or not they knew he was behind them.
They turned in unison.
'Sorry old geezer,' the first apologised, 'but me blood is up!' At that the lift pinged and came to a sudden stop. The orderlies exited first, their conversation unchanged, faded as they walked away.
The garden was peaceful. A small water feature trickled in the corner. Reynolds watched it for some time. Like liquid metal, he thought, translucent white and slow to pour. It reminded him of mercury and the chemistry classes at school. Mrs Downey had taken him for chemistry. He almost wondered what she was up to now, before remembering that she must have died decades ago.
The garden was small and completely surrounded on all sides by the five floors of the hospital. There were a couple of benches on square concrete slabs, a small wooden table, and a rectangle of grass. A few shrubs grew up at the edges against the hospital walls. There were probably flowers in the summer, he thought, but not now. He missed his cats.
Looking up at the windows that looked down on him, Reynolds imagined the various scenes played out in each room -

sad scenes, happy scenes, perverse scenes, scenes witnessed by the living and scenes witnessed by the dead. He imagined the inhabitants of the hospital as simian; the doctors were gorillas, the nurses chimps, and the patients, well, they were howlers, screaming at dusk and dawn. He saw them hanging out of the windows, climbing down the drainpipes. They were out of control, lustful, shameless, animal.

A gorilla stepped into the garden, disturbing his thoughts. The great ape pulled a cigarette from its pocket, struck a match and inhaled deeply. The blue smoke hung in the air. The old man wondered if different breeds of monkey and ape could communicate with each other – was it worth him asking his simian brother for a cigarette? He decided against it.

The gorilla's eyes were heavy and ringed by thick black shadows, it groaned unconsciously each time it exhaled. The white coat it was wearing was smeared with streaks of a red brown liquid. There was evidence of solid matter encrusted within the smears – bits of food or flesh, Reynolds reasoned. The gorilla finished its cigarette and went back inside, shaking its furry head as it did so.

Reynolds turned up the thick collar of his dressing gown. The night air was cold. He wished he'd brought his pipe along. He was trying to give up, Dr Knowles had advised him to, but it's hard to break the habit of a lifetime. He sat on the bench furthest from the water feature and looked up at the night sky. No stars were visible through the pollution of hospital lights and the black sky looked more orange than anything else, the sort of orange you get at dusk – thick and wispy with thin threads of grey. He felt like a goldfish in a goldfish bowl.

The following two days were as uneventful as the preceding ones. He got no news from the silverback Doc Fleming concerning his scans and his neighbour continued howling at the nursing staff for a more potent fix. He read one of the books his son brought in, but the boy was so unimaginative in his choices that Reynolds couldn't face the others.

The 'Friends of William Harvey' brought the papers round daily. They were a religious lot, like any group or club with the title 'Friends of…' He had noticed that all religious males wore soft-soled leather loafers, usually light brown or tan in colour. This contradicted the accepted notion of the sandal, or the Jesus creeper. It did however confirm that God prefers soft souls. He imagined the disciples at the last supper, looking suspiciously at Judas with his Oxblood Doc Martins. So, it had been nine days since his last blackout, nine very laborious days.

Outside his window the autumn sun hung low in the crisp blue sky. There were a few vapour trails and the odd cirrus cloud, both stretching and fragmenting until they appeared like the bones of some great fish suspended above 24,000 feet.

The old man rested his arms on the plastic windowsill and made hot breath patterns on the glass.

He had decided the previous night that today would be his last day in this morgue. The great apes obviously had no idea what was wrong with him; the constipation medication was completely ineffective and he missed his cats too much to remain any longer. The books his son had brought in he would leave in the window-bay; he was sure someone would be interested in them. Apart from his pyjamas and toothbrush, all he had was the clothes he came in.

Reynolds would be ready to leave at 6pm once he had imbibed some of the foul dinner they served to the old and infirm.

Six o'clock.

Reynolds had only managed to eat a couple of lukewarm boiled potatoes. He hated boiled potatoes but the chicken that accompanied them was so dry that he feared he would be unable to swallow it, or even worse choke and that would definitely scupper his plans.

Everything was packed and ready in the carrier bag he'd brought it in. He had his clothes on underneath his dressing gown and kept his slippers on, so as not too attract attention. He would change into his coat and shoes once he was downstairs in the public area, he could use the visitors' toilets for that.

The nurses took their break after the evening meal was cleared away, leaving only one nurse to man the station at the end of the corridor. That, he decided, was his opportunity.

Firstly he took his bag of clothes into the toilet and put them in a cubicle, it was only a short walk from there to the nurses' station and he would be able to retrieve them quickly. Next he approached the nurse at the station.

The chimp was sitting at the desk reading a chart, his chin resting on his hand, his breathing heavy with boredom. He did not hear the old man approach.

'Sorry to disturb you nurse.' Reynolds said. The chimp's tired eyes rotated upwards. 'It's just I think the gentleman in the room next to mine is in some difficulty. I could hear him coughing and…I don't know he just sounded like he was having trouble breathing.'

The nurse raised his eyebrows and pouted – a moment's silence passed between them.

'Well,' he said, 'I can't hear anything now.'

This was unexpected. 'Well, erm, no.' Reynolds stumbled, 'But he was definitely in some distress.'

The primate exhaled noisily blowing out his large floppy lips as he did so. 'Thank you Mr Reynolds.' he said, his words accompanied by a condescending smile.

Another awkward silence hung in the space between them. Reynolds waited. He thought the ape would do something: hang from the light fitting, beat his hairy chest, and bellow loudly… something. But he did nothing, save return to his boredom and the chart on the desk in front of him.

Reynolds turned and made his way down the corridor.

'Arsehole!' he cursed, under his breath.

Back in his room he re-evaluated the situation. There had to be something he could do?

After a few moments thought, Reynolds nodded. 'It is the only option,' he mumbled, running his hand over his bald scalp. There was nothing else for it.

Checking the corridor was clear, Reynolds moved stealthily toward his neighbour's room. He didn't bother to knock but opened the door and entered in one impressively fluid movement – like a panther through the jungle.

Mr Long was lying on his back, his eyes closed, the big red button gripped desperately in his claw like hand. Reynolds tiptoed around the bed; he didn't want the junky to wake. The nurse call button, his goal, was hanging on the metallic headrest. It was attached to a long wire, very similar to the morphine remote. Reynolds plucked it from its position.

The next bit was the trickiest. Mr Long was a desperate man; he had seen it in his eyes a few days ago. The old man would have to be very gentle.

Bending over the bed he sized up the options available. If he were to remove the morphine release button in one go it would mean a single, but powerful tug, more than likely resulting in Mr Long's sudden awakening. But if he were to try and remove it slowly…

Reynolds gripped the wire; one short sharp movement should do it, he thought, and tugged. The button came free landing on the bed covers; at that moment the old man shoved the nurse call button in its place. He didn't wait to see if Long had awoken because it really didn't matter. If he had woken he would push the button, if he hadn't, he would push it sooner rather than later anyway. Either way the old man got what he wanted.

Within five minutes Mr Long needed a fix.

The emergency buzzer was just audible through the wall. Reynolds waited until he heard the slap, slap, slap of the chimp's footsteps. He stood with the door to his room open only a crack and watched the unenthusiastic male nurse enter Long's room. Then, in a flash he was out the door. He quickly grabbed his clothes from the toilet cubicle and made off toward the lifts.

The stairwell was a safer route otherwise he might have to wait for the lift to arrive. It's only three floors, he thought, and down at that. The plastic carrier bag knocked against his leg as he descended, his fingers hooked loosely round the banister. He passed nobody.

Reynolds pushed through the double doors into the public lounge. The public toilets were to his right; he would have to negotiate the various sales desks planted there to snare the recently bereaved, or recently released. They didn't close up shop until visiting hours were over at 8pm.

He imagined himself standing in the middle of the room naked, his erect penis pointing at the smarmy, sickly salesmen and women like a 45 automatic. They have their hands up and he shoots them with great globs of semen, in the mouth and eyes. They run screaming, the juice burning their false human flesh revealing the steaming, scheming alien beneath. That is how we will tell the simian/humans apart, he thinks; they will be immune to the body's ammunition.

Head down, Reynolds made his move. Luckily the aliens at the first two desks were talking to each other in their 'off world' tongue.

'O.M.G. that's barking!' exclaimed the female, twisting her blond extensions.

'Yeah, bro didn't know,' the male confirmed, nodding his oversized head and making the strangest of hand movements.

The next desk was dead.

The fourth desk was advertising various cut-price funeral arrangements. A poster of a mourning family and extravagant caskets were pinned on the display board with the words DIGNITY and PEACE in large black letters. The woman sitting at the desk had the grey expression of a pallbearer. She smiled at Reynolds, wrinkling her terrible features. Reynolds looked down at the floor.

He took little notice of the others peddling their wares and ignored one man's lure of an, 'Exclusive Holiday' with every purchase over five hundred pounds.

The public toilets were empty. Reynolds found a cubicle and changed into his coat and shoes. His stomach twisted, sending pain through his intestine. Reynolds pulled down his trousers and sat on the toilet seat.

Whether it was nerves, or the thought of going home, he didn't know, but for the first time in nine days he managed to shit. It wasn't much, just a concrete nugget or two, but the relief was overwhelming. Reynolds smiled.

All done he washed the stench of the morgue from his face and hands and took a long gulp of water from the basin tap. He smiled at the mirror, now the colour was beginning to return to his face.

The old man passed through reception without being noticed; he was just another visitor leaving. There was lightness to his steps now, like walking on the moon he thought, they were no longer the movements of a man interred. The gorillas, chimps and howlers were too busy with their own business to bother with him and he was soon on the path leading away from the main building.

He remembered a shortcut to Holbourne Lane, a pathway that took you round by the nurses' quarters and through a small coppice of evergreen trees. He only knew about this from when his wife was ill. His son would drive to see her but refused to pay the fees for hospital parking. In Holbourne Lane, parking was free for an hour and there were usually plenty of spaces. From there it was easy enough to make it to the main road. He would be home within an hour.

At the end of Holbourne Lane you can see over the whole town, contained, as it is, in what appears to be a huge meteorite crater.

Reynolds stood for a moment with the sounds of the town drifting up and over him. On the motorway, the diamonds and rubies of speeding traffic blinked as they passed tree and fence and other cars. Blue lights flashed and the piecing wail of a siren washed over him, distilled by the distance between them.

The scene reminded him of Paris, standing atop the Montparnasse tower watching the city traffic fifty-nine stories below. He had joined a tourist tour, with his hip flask of whisky and a pack of Gitanes in his pocket. He ate escargots and partridge that night in a nice little Latin Quarter bistro near the Sorbonne.

During his working life Reynolds had visited most of the major cities in Europe, but Paris was by far his favourite, closely followed by Amsterdam. The old man closed his eyes.

BLACKOUT!

Reynolds opened his eyes to a different world from the one before. The diamonds and rubies continued on their path but everything else was black and formless. Darker shadows' within the blackness held no definition and a streaking wisp of grey, like the tail of a ghost, wove random fading patterns.

The entire town was blacked out. He could hear alarms in the distance running on battery power, triggered by the sudden outage. Holbourne Lane was completely dark. In the houses around him the flicker of candlelight and faint torch beams began to appear. Children shrieked, excited by the surprise of it all and people began to emerge from their dark houses. Reynolds took his leave heading down Pretor Hill towards home.

It was colder in the darkness and Reynolds wished he had left his dressing gown on beneath his coat. He turned up his collar and fastened the pop studs around his neck. His son had told him to take a jumper but the old man was resistant to any orders given by that little shit.

The paths were badly maintained along the main road, to discourage pedestrians from using them – the Government wanted everyone to travel by car, so that they would pay road tax and fill their coffers. In the darkness the paths were almost impossible, when a car approached, its lights were blinding and on several occasion Reynolds buckled his ankle and stubbed his toe . He turned into Manson Avenue; he could take a short cut through the park, he thought. It might cut fifteen minutes off the journey. The incessant bleep and buzz of burglar alarms attacked his ears. More and more people appeared on the street now – some just out walking in the darkness, while others were checking out how far the blackout actually spread. Most were carrying torches, most were holding hands, some had their dogs on leads and others didn't.

Ragnor Park was quieter – not many people and no burglar alarms. Reynolds followed the path through the small wooded area. He felt sure no one else would be that brave. Twigs and leaves snapped and crackled underfoot, a reassuring sound he thought. Then his ears tuned into another sound, quite subtle and at some distance; but it was definitely there. Something like a four-legged creature, he thought, perhaps a dog, or a cat? He clapped his hands, if it was a dog it would surely run at that – they're all cowards at heart. But the noise remained. He stopped and listened. It wasn't a cat, not a domestic cat anyway. A cold shiver ran the length of his spine.

There had been reports of strange creatures living on the hills surrounding the town, the usual tales of panthers and lynx taking sheep and chickens, scaring holiday walkers and enraging local farmers. It was quite possible that these creatures would come into town to feed on smaller cats and foxes and dogs. The old man tried to penetrate the darkness. It would be a real honour to see one of these creatures, he thought, if a little terrifying.

A twig snapped. Reynolds turned quickly; a rush of leaves followed this, and he thought he saw a pair of yellow-green eyes in the darkness. His breathing increased, fight or flight, fight or flight? The old man chose flight.

Within a few minutes he was out in the open, near the football pitches and tennis courts. He heard voices on the path in front of him and slowed his pace to a brisk walk, his heavy breaths wheezing audibly.

A group of teenagers passed him, smoking a joint. They made no effort to disguise the fact and Reynolds made no comment. They were heading for the woods, prey for the hunter therein.

Not far now. Naseby Avenue was next; so he was nearly home. He checked his coat for his house keys, something he should have done at the hospital. They jingled.

The cats would be pleased to see him, as he would them. There were some treats in the kitchen cupboard they all enjoyed. A nice cup of tea, he thought. Yes, a treat for the cats and some Malted Milk biscuits for him. He would have to go shopping tomorrow; he could do that in the morning and then spend the afternoon in front of the telly. It would be nice to doze on the sofa again, a man misses his little luxuries when they are denied him.

Naseby Avenue into Wellington into Waterloo Road. The neighbourhood smelled familiar. He took the back alley that runs from Waterloo Road to St Martins. A dog barked and scratched at a wooden panelled fence.

'Shut up!' Reynolds barked in return, the dog paid him no heed.

Down St Martins then left into Royal Military.

Approaching his house he scanned for his son's car. He thought he might be waiting for him. There was no sign of it.

The blackout had played into his hands. The hospital was probably too busy seeing to the emergency cases to worry about someone going AWOL. His son probably didn't even know yet.

Turning the key he pushed through the door. Immediately the kittens appeared. He still referred to them as kittens even though they were nearly as big as Jasper. They purred round his legs, rubbing themselves against his shins as he shut and bolted the door behind him. Reynolds bent down and grabbed one in each arm. They purred and nuzzled lovingly, rubbing their faces against him.

The old man called for Jasper and Leila, but there was no response. He went into the kitchen, put down the kittens and unlocked the back door. As soon as it was opened Jasper appeared.

Reynolds scooped him up. Jasper's purr soon drowns out the kittens. The old man rubbed his finger around Jasper's neck.

Leila sauntered in a few minutes later. She made her usual fuss and then went over to the food bowls mewing. Lotty and Leaky were close behind.

It was while Reynolds was waiting for his saucepan of water to boil that he heard a car screech to a halt outside. He moved into the front room. Sure enough there was his son getting out of his Audi, all hot and bothered. Oh the stress of having to look after a cantankerous old man! He watched as the boy looked at the house, searching for signs of habitation.

'This will be interesting,' Reynolds mumbled, glad that he had bolted the front door. Then, picking up the kittens, both of which had followed him into the room, he smiled and walked back into the kitchen. Nobody was going to take him back into that morgue.

——ooOoo——

Tim Goss lives and works in Folkestone

JOEY'S

Penelope Gotch

Tom hated the alleyway. He hated how it was cold, dark and damp, and how it stank of piss, puke and garbage, but most of all, he hated the flickering neon sign on the wall that said 'Joey's'. It didn't need to say more: everybody knew Joey nowadays. If you wanted Rapture, you went to him.

Tom parked his motorbike, climbed off, hesitated. He didn't want to leave it there where any stupid drunk could just drive off with it, but he didn't have a choice. You never did with Joey.

He opened the door and walked through.

Inside was darker than out. Tom couldn't see a thing. For all he knew, Joey could be standing an inch from his face, or the room could be completely empty. There was no way to tell.

'Hello?'

A desk lamp clicked on. Its light was bright enough after the gloom to make Tom squint and briefly shield his eyes. Behind the desk on which the lamp stood sat Joey, elbows resting on the dull metal and fingers laced, looking the same as always: same slicked-down silver hair, same black suit, same wire-framed glasses, and same shady smile that made Tom feel sick.

'Thomas. Good evening.'

'You got it?'

Joey arched an eyebrow, its curve a dark slash against his pale forehead. 'No pleasantries! Have you my payment?'

'Yes. Have you got *it*?'

'Maybe I have, and maybe I don't have.' Joey leant back in his chair, put his arms behind his head and grinned. 'Show me the money, Thomas.'

The threat of a scowl made Tom's facial muscles twitch, but he fought it: he took a deep breath, counted to ten, and breathed out again. It was what his mother always told him to do when he was young, before the Crisis, before she died. Losing your temper with Joey never helped. You had to stay calm.

Tom slipped a hand into his pocket, pulled out a crumpled piece of olive-green paper, and dropped it onto Joey's desk.

It was a pre-Crisis American one-dollar bill. Tom had begged, borrowed, bribed, scared, stolen and struck to get it, and it had taken him three weeks.

Joey snatched the bill up and thrust it under the lamp light, leaning in close, poring over its surface. Tom hugged his arms around his narrow chest and resisted the urge to tap his foot with impatience. He'd broken his back to get what Joey asked for: now he wanted his reward.

Joey folded the note in half, tucked it into his breast pocket and looked up expectantly. Tom stared back. Blank.

'What?'

'Where's the rest?'

Tom's heart started to beat harder against his ribs. He could hear the rush of its pulse in his hears and the tingling of its surge in his fingers. A dull roar began to rise in the base of his skull.

;What do you mean *the rest*? This is all you asked for!' Joey shook his head. Laughed.

'Prices rise, kid.'

He pulled a plastic bag out of his jacket pocket. Inside were half a dozen pills, small and shiny and pure white. Rapture tablets: swallow one of those and the Crisis became a distant, half-remembered nightmare and the world went back to what it should be. Everybody wanted them. Everybody needed them. Tom needed them.

There was a round green sticky label on the bag: $4.95.Tom tried to count to ten again, but his thoughts were snarled like fraying wool. He ran a hand through his short dark hair and found it damp with sweat.

'I can't pay that, Joe.'

'But that's the price. Take it or leave it.'

Tom swore under his breath and bit his lip. He could walk away, give up. Except that this was *Rapture*. He'd do anything to get it. Had done almost anything to get it. He *needed* it.

'Dollar fifty?'

'Oh *please*, Thomas.'

'Dollar ninety-five, then.'

Joey stood up, chair scraping across the floor, and put the bag back in his pocket before sidling around the desk, cracking each of his knuckles individually as he went. Tom folded his arms again and stood firm. His hands were almost vibrating with energy and his stomach was twisting, but he refused to run. Not even from tough jerks a foot taller than and twice as wide as him.

Joey pushed his glasses up his nose with an elegant finger.

'I do *not* haggle. Pay up, or get out.'

'Fine, *fine*. Gimme my money back, then.'

Joey laughed again, that infuriating laugh, and shook his head.

'No refunds, Thomas. *Shoo.*'

The anger clouding Tom's thoughts distilled into bright clear rage as sharp as broken dreams. He knew what to do. He swung a punch at Joey's face. Joey caught his wrist and twisted it backwards until it cracked. Tom gasped and tried to pull away, but the grip was too tight, too strong, and Joey pulled him in close enough to whisper "You stupid little *fool*. Too bad for you." And he drove his knee into Tom's stomach.

Tom dropped, retched, gasped, the air driven from his lungs. The world blurred into kick after kick after kick, to his back, his ribs, his stomach, his head, everywhere, and he curled into a ball, hands over his head, praying Joey would stop. And finally, he did.

Tom's body hurt. Breathing hurt. *Living* hurt. Rough fingers grabbed the back of Tom's grey woolly jumper and pulled him to his feet. He staggered against Joey, fingers darting in and out of a jacket pocket a bare moment before Joey shoved him away, kicked him in the back of the knee, then threw him bodily out the door.

Tom landed hard, rolled, scrambled to his feet, his fists clenched to his face. The alleyway was *filthy* and Joey had thrown him right into the filth as though he was nothing but garbage. Joey, who stood silhouetted in the doorway, arms folded.

'Ready to apologise?'

'Drop dead!'

Tom spat at Joey's feet and dived for his motorbike. Joey snarled with anger and darted forward, but Tom was too quick: he flipped up the kickstand, revved the engine and roared off, a torrent of abuse following him and speed limits shattered in his wake.

BUT THAT DIDN'T MATTER. None of it mattered. Not Joey, not the insults, not even the pain. All that mattered was the little bag of pills in his hand and the single thought that was whirling around his head: *I won.*

——ooOoo——

Penny Gotch was born in Luton in 1991. Raised in Essex, she now lives in Folkestone, Kent, where she is studying a Creative & Professional Writing degree. "Joey's" is her first published short story, but her poem "Of Another World" was featured in "Asperger United Magazine", and she was one of ten winners in the poetry stage of the Poets & Muses competition run by Gentleman Press. Penny also enjoys reading, baking and playing video games.

A FIRESIDE TALE
(For Four Northumbrian Voices)

Margaret Harland-Suddes

Seagulls calling and sounds of waves breaking

    MALE VOICE
A fisherwife once lived in Cullercoats,
A comely woman, pillar of her church.
She had but one son Jack, her only joy,
A braw, brave and a bonny lad he was.
From childhood he had sailed the coble-boats,
'longside his father, learnt the fisher's craft;
The sea was in his blood, he knew no fear;
To be a fisherman his one desire,
And live in Cullercoats his only dream.

    FEMALE VOICE
Their peaceful days came to a cruel end,
When war clouds overshadowed all the land;
The fisherwife was grieved, when he was called
To be a naval rating in that war.
Her heart was overwhelmed with fear and dread;
But she had faith, and trusted in her prayers.
God was her refuge in her time of need;
The saints would keep Jack safe and bring him home.

MALE VOICE
All through the Kaiser's war, Jack fought at sea
Right bravely, and won medals in the fray.
The war kept him from home, for four long years,
Crossing the oceans, serving his country's need.
His letters told how much he missed his home,
That he was well, and she was dearly loved.
He wrote of battles that his ship had fought;
He'd been at Scapa Flow, with Jellicoe,
And fought at Jutland, 'gainst the German Fleet.
Then Armistice, was signed; Great God be praised!
The war was ended, soon Jack would come home.
When all the guns fell silent, Jack's ship sailed,
To bring him home, and light her life again.

FEMALE VOICE
Most tragically, the vessel it was lost.
Somewhere beneath the North Atlantic deeps
It struck a floating mine and quickly sank.
"Lost with all hands" the official papers said..
She couldn't read the telegram for tears;
Would not believe the words, when she was told;
Ran screaming from the house like one possessed.
Tearing her hair, she fled into the church;
Distraught, she knelt before the altar rail,
Wringing her hands; beseeching Heaven to hear.

WIFE *(pleading and with emotion)*
Dear Father, let him live; let Jack come home.
He is the only joy you've given to me.
I beg you not to part me from my son;
Dear God, please give him back and let him live.

MALE VOICE
The hollow building echoed to her prayer,

As over and again she said the words.
But never an answering word came from on high;
No angel flew to earth to comfort her.
The church lay silent; no one heard her plea.
The saints stood in their niches deaf and dumb;
And parson was far away across the fells,
Visiting the farms, before the snows set in.

    FEMALE VOICE
They found her in the dark at eventide,
Prostrate and cold upon the altar steps;
Scarcely alive, her heartbeat fluttering faint.
Her husband carried her home, fearing she would die.
Her heart was broken; she'd no will to live.
Her mind unhinged, by her most grievous loss;
She fell into a fever of the brain,
Rambling in her talk, no longer sane.
Her husband, good man that he was, he tried
To comfort her, but nothing quenched her grief,
So sunken was she in her black despair;
Raving, she'd never again see her dear boy.
In melancholic despair, she wept and pined,
Until her husband and her friends believed
That she would die, before the year's end came.

    MALE VOICE
All winter long, he nursed her, kept her safe
And tried to cheer her heart and make her smile.
They'd sit together, warm beside the fire,
But all the light that lit her eyes had died.
Her hair had lost its sheen and when she spoke
Her voice was feeble, like a little child.
Her husband, was gentle with her, did his best,
But it was clear, her soul was in decline.

WIFE *(weakly and confused)*
I heard a wailing in the air last night.

HUSBAND *(kindly)*
Dear lass, you heard the wind across the moor.

WIFE *(startled)*
Who comes a-tapping on the window-pane?

HUSBAND
It's but the rattling rain and nothing more.

WIFE *(fearfully)*
Someone lies hiding, spying by the gate.

HUSBAND *(trying to cheer her.)*
There's nothing near the gate but yellow furze;
You used to dye Jack's pace-eggs with the flowers.
D'ye not ken how he liked bright-coloured eggs?
You'd wrap old onion skins around them tight
And boil them, so they'd come out golden brown.

WIFE. *(in a resigned voice)*
When Easter comes, Jack will be safely home,
And I will boil him pace eggs like before.

FEMALE VOICE
She twined her arms around her knees, and rocked
Backward and forth upon the creaking stool,
Picturing those happy days when he was young.
They seemed like some faint dream from long ago.

WIFE *(sadly)*
Today, while I was baking, the fire was quenched
And all my batch of "singin' hinnies" were spoilt.

HUSBAND *(gently)*
The rain came down the chimney, bonny lass,
And water drenched the coals; the fire went out.
What makes you fear someone is taunting you?

WIFE *(tearfully)*
Because God has forsaken me, turned His back,
And now the Devil's imps tease me each day.
The war is over; Jack should be at home;
'Tis God Himself that keeps my bairn away.
I pleaded for His help; He closed His ears.
    (she begins to weep)

HUSBAND *(softly to console her)*
It grieves my heart, dear lass, to see you sad;
Jack is not hidden; our son is dead and gone;
We have our memories from happier times.
God did not choose to bring this grief on you.
One day we both will see his face again.

FEMALE VOICE
She covered up her ears and screamed and cri

WIFE *(confused and angry)*
I will not hear you say my Jack is dead.
He`s on the sea, somewhere, and coming home.
Sometimes I hear his footsteps on the path.
But when I run to see, they draw him back
And keep him hidden, to hold him from my side.

HUSBAND *(sadly and softly, to calm her)*
There are no footsteps on the gravel path;
You hear the crashing waves down by the shore.

WIFE *(eagerly)*
Today I found some seashells on the step;
Jack always brings shells back when he comes home.

HUSBAND *(interrupting her)*
Those shells are old, they've lain there many years,
He brought them from the beach when he was small.

WIFE *(ignoring him, excitedly.)*
Husband, I know our boy will soon come home ...

HUSBAND *(trying to calm her)*
He cannot come sweet lass, he's fathoms deep.

WIFE *(excited, still ignoring him)*
I've made his bed; it's soft, for his return.
Surely, he will be back when Easter comes.

HUSBAND *(sadly and resigned)*
How can he come, when death has closed his eyes?

WIFE *(shouting at him)*
He does not sleep, and soon he will be here!

MALE VOICE
In such mad grieving, slowly the dark days passed. *(pauses)*
The autumn and winter brought rough seas and gales;
The coble-boats could seldom put to sea.
The fishing was poor; the herring shoals stayed off,
Feeding in water deeper than men could fish.
Then came a turning of the wrecking winds,
The herring at last, came nearer to the shore.
Out on the cliffs the look-outs ran to tell;

Great silver swathes were feeding close inshore.
The fishermen prepared to bring them in.
Great God be praised, the herring shoals were back!
The coble boats sailed out, *to fish the banks,
And Cullercoats bustled with fishing, once again.

    FEMALE VOICE
That herring harvest was the best for years.
And heavy creels of fish, were brought ashore.
The women gathered, when the boats came in;
Their gutting knives already sharp and bright;
It was their work to split and salt the catch,
Prepare the fish, and fill the smoke-house racks.
The smell of smouldering oak chips fumed the air,
Curing those laden catches from the sea.
The women toiled till dark, down on the beach,
Scraping the scaly herring, every day,
Their stinking clothes splattered with silver scales,
Their hands, red-raw, from wind and brine and fish.
But there was happy laughter on the shore,
For hard work was the only life they knew.
Then, cured and boxed, the kippers were carted south.
Such was the way the fishers earned their pay.

    MALE VOICE
The fisherwife walked endlessly alone,
Shunning, all company, work, and village life.
The anguished weeks had brought a gloomy change;
An air of darkness hung about her now.
She seldom said a word to anyone;
Neglected her wifely duties every day,
Wandered instead upon the cliffs or shore,
Listening for voices whispering on the wind,
Seeking mysterious messages, none could give.

     FEMALE VOICE
When Shrovetide and Lent were ended, church bells rang;
The nave was decked in brightest springtime flowers.
Easter had come, and Christ the Lord was risen.
The Cullercoats fisherfolk sang joyfully in praise.
The harvest of the sea, His bounteous gift,
Had filled their nets. They gladly sang and prayed.

     MALE VOICE
Each year, at Eastertime, a pedlar came
With laden baskets tricked-out with pretty things.
Then all the village buzzed, with laughing wives
And dancing maids flocking to buy such treats.

     MALE and FEMALE VOICES *(alternately, with excitement)*
A ribbon for the hair; a length of lace;
A tin-plate toy, a bobbin of silk thread,
Pearl buttons for a waistcoat newly stitched,
A dainty collar of embroidered voile,
New cuffs to brighten up a tired gown,
A measuring tape hidden in a white whalebone,
Red spotted kerchief, combs to hold the hair.

     FEMALE VOICE *(interrupting)*
The good man tried to tempt his wife with treats
But she just shook her head, and dumbly stared;
Until she spied a penny whistle shine
Beneath the gaudy ribbons and twists of lace.
That was the only thing her heart desired.
Her boy had often played to make her smile.
He'd pipe a jig or rousing marching song.
Her soulful-eyes begged only one penny piece,
Her one desire, to learn to pipe a tune.

MALE VOICE
Her husband could not deny such simple joy;
And gladly bought the penny pipe for her.
Then, with a kiss, bestowed the favoured toy,
Told her, she was his own fair, bonny lass.
It pleased him well that she should want to play.
He'd give the world, if only she would smile.

FEMALE VOICE
The fisherwife went wandering on the shore;
She cared not what the other women said.
They had their bairns about them safe at home;
She, only a gnawing, emptiness in her breast.
Each day she paced the lowest ebb-tide reach,
That lay beyond the turning tidal flow.
Her neighbours marked her aimless wanderings,
Unhinged by grief and muttering to herself,
Pausing each now and then to face the wind,
Turn to each quarter (North, South, West and East),
Blow shrilly on her pipe some strange, harsh tune,
Pause, listen intently; cast her gaze to sea,
Willing her dear, sweet boy to come to her.

MALE VOICE
For seven long days she scarcely left the shore,
Keeping her lonely vigil, night and day,
Until her husband questioned why she stayed
So long out of the house, and by the sea.

WIFE *(in a simple and matter-of-fact voice)*
I'm whistling-up a wind to bring Jack home.

MALE VOICE
She answered simply, turning her mournful gaze.

HUSBAND *(with deep concern)*
God help us, Woman, when will this madness end?
No fisherwoman whistles for the wind.
Such wicked business stands against God's laws.
The dead must rest in peace, until He calls.
'Tis by God's Grace some sleep in hallowed ground
And many a fisherman rests beneath the sea.
God gives them each a place to lie, and wait.
Do not oppose that awful, solemn law,
For nothing but evil comes from such a deed.

WIFE *(shrilly and with rising anger)*
What care I for God`s laws? I seek my child;
And I will whistle till he comes to me.
I've lived my life in keeping with God`s will,
And bowed my head to every burden given.
One child alone was all the joy I knew,
I will not yield him up to Hell or Heaven.
If God wills that my only son be dead,
Then, I am left to make a Devil's pact,
So Jack may be with me, and I with him.
I care not for the laws of God or man.
I'll whistle in every quarter, at low tide,
For I believe he'll hear his mother's call.
North, South, East, West; my son will hear my cry;
He`ll come to me again, though God forbids.
(She changes her tone; softly and with affection)
He was a good bairn, always came when called,
No matter how far, or what the game he played.
And now, he will not fail to heed my pipe,
Keening into the wind to beckon him.
(with rising determination and power.)
Oh, I will whistle loud as Gabriel`s horn,
And Jack will hear me with his loving heart.
Through storm or tempest, he will find a way;

Though legions of devils bar the way, he'll come.
He will not keep from me, and see me pine.
Full seven tides, I've whistled for the wind;
And seven times I've cursed the heavens on high,
Broken the holy laws, that fisherfolk all keep,
    (shrilly and in tearful desperation)
So, come he must ...OR I WILL DROWN AT SEA!

    HUSBAND *(deeply distressed, trying to calm her.)*
Dear wife, why must you seek to fight God's will?
Our son lies lost; his soul is gone from him.
He cannot waken now till Judgment Day;
His bones are whitened in his deep-sea grave.

    WIFE *(forcefully, and with angry determination)*
Then I will whistle, till the Devil hears;
I`ll pipe and whistle, face whatever comes.
Between the tides I'll hunt till Hell is breached;
Do what I must; I've sworn to find my boy ...

    MALE   VOICE
When dawn's first rays came glimmering in the sky,
She quietly stole across the silent shore,
And loosed Jack's coble-boat into the tide,
Hoisted the flapping sail to catch the wind,
Then sailed, fearless of danger, out to sea.
A light breeze ruffled white caps on the waves,
As into the mist, the fisherwife steered far.
No one saw any sign of how she left;
Her good-man slept, so lightly did she leave.
An evil wind came whistling from the North,
And carried her beyond the harbour-bar.
She steadied the boat and shrieked into the wind.

WIFE *(shrieking madly)*
Hear me dear lad! I've come to call you back!
Rise up, come sit beside me and we'll sail.
For I am willing to leave this world behind
And roam the seas with you, beyond God's grace.
For you, I'll forfeit my immortal soul,
Relinquish Salvation, sup with the Devil himself,
And be an outcast, till Eternity.

FEMALE VOICE
She lashed the sail, and took the pipe again,
Whistling her strange tune wildly to the sky.
Tumultuous waves rose high; wild storm-clouds surged;
As though in answer to her anguished plea.
Tears streamed down from her eyes, till she was blind.
Her tossing boat ploughed swiftly on its way,
Carrying her afar on mountainous waves;
But piping madly, she felt naught of fear.
Fair visions of her son were in her mind,
She felt his presence, singing in the storm.
A pall of weird, blue-lightning, struck the boat;
Her loosened hair, streamed out into the wind.
Then, in a phosphorescent flash, she saw
Jack's smiling face, all strange and ghastly white,
Rising towards her, from the hellish deeps;
Reaching his arms to touch her where she sat.

WIFE *(grief-stricken, and tearful)*
Oh son, dear son, come to your mother's arms,
As once you did, when you were but a child ...

MALE VOICE *(interrupting)*
High on the cliffs, men hunting, watched the scene.
The parson, the farmer and the local squire.
They, hurrying homeward to escape the storm,

High, from the headland, witnessed what befell.
Watched, through a spyglass, the grim sights at sea,
Transfixed, but too far off to render help;
No means lay anywhere to save those souls. *(pause, sadly.)*
When all had passed too far for mortal help,
They hurried home agog, to tell their tale.
A coble heading outward, northward driven,
Its red sail set full-on, into the storm.
Making no effort to turn for leeward shores;
Seeming to steer a course straight for Hell`s mouth,
Dangerously buffeted by the Devil`s own glee,
Driven on, as they could see, without remorse.
Cape Horn could never have raged a wilder sea.
Hell's maw gaped wide, to draw the coble in,
While stinking, sulphurous fumes poisoned the air.
And strangely to their eyes, they each agree,
At first there was but one who manned the oars,
Then, of a sudden, two sat side by side,
Both rowing, oblivious of those monstrous waves
And, keeping their steady unison, all unfazed,
Pulling in rhythm, easy and content,
Skimming the angry sea, as in a skiff,
Laughing, as though they picnicked on a lake,
Seated in mortal danger, without a care,
A woman with a young man at her side,
Bathed in a strange, and eerie, livid glow
That spoke, to those who watched, of some strange power
Drawing the tragic pair on to their fate.

FEMALE VOICE
The parson spent long hours upon his knees
Praying for both the souls lost to the sea.
But village folk said it was the Devil's work,
And all the Cullercoats fisherfolk agreed:

No godly woman whistles for a wind
To change the natural order wrought by death.
Such wickedness denies God's holy will,
And those who bargain for the Devil's boon,
Pay with their immortal souls the Devil's price.

    MALE VOICE
The strange story was told, down through the years
By witnesses of worth, who'd seen those things.
No answers were found to solve the strange affair.
No bodies floated home to any shore.
No wreckage of the coble, ever found.

    FEMALE VOICE
Some said that Jack came back to ease her grief.
Some vowed her whistling opened Hell's grim gates.
But many of the fisher folk believe
To whistle the Devil's wind flies in God's face.
To cheat the dead their grave is mortal sin.

(Sea sounds, and call of sea-gulls......fading out.)
        ——ooOoo——

Margaret Harland-Suddes came down to Folkestone from Durham in 1973 with her late husband, two children, several qualifications from Durham University, and a fellowship from the College of Teachers, to take up a post as founding head of Palmarsh C.P. School which she held for 20 years before taking early retirement. She has had a lifelong interest in Art and Creative Writing (prose and poetry) as well as writing and producing school plays and musicals

THE AFTERLIFE OF STEPHEN BALLS

Briony Kapoor

There are occasions when the Lord God and the Lord Satan meet on neutral ground to review those cases of souls whose destination after leaving this brief life is not entirely clear. On one such occasion the two Lords were sitting at a long plain table when the question of the resting place of Stephen Balls arose. Paying scant attention to the task but preoccupied with their thoughts the two each found their meetings to have a quality of intensity not provided by the general aeon of eternity. A frisson of a different kind occurred when they extended their arms to shake hands after the completion of work. A degree of mutual respect close to affection existed between the great lords. Nevertheless, their palms could not actually touch as the opposing forces of good and evil emanating therefrom exerted an antipathetic force that prevented the mingling of their principal qualities. A useful safeguard that prevented the sort of moral muddle that had once resulted in the creation of mixed up humanity – a species that could never afterwards sort out the issues of good and evil satisfactorily amongst themselves.

Whenever the Lord God and the Lord Satan were together there was also the risk that each might catch, in the eye of the other, a gleam indicating mutual acknowledgment and possibly even enjoyment of their unique and powerful position. An acknowledgment of equality was to the benefit of neither. Tempting as the communication might seem, both tried to avoid it. A dangerous moment of this kind had just occurred when the matter pertaining to Balls came under scrutiny. The note by which they were to judge read that he was a ruthless businessman.

"Sounds like one of yours," said God

"He doesn't seem to have done anything spectacularly bad," responded Satan, "but I could take him into purgatory, I suppose, if you have that rather miserable do-gooder, whose case is also confusing, in exchange."

And it was agreed that this should be so.

The passage of time is uncertain in the afterlife but it is sure that, before long, Stephen Balls, a man of great determination and energy, was buying and selling areas of the infernal regions. He had several of the smaller and more easily influenced devils under his command and they were already mobilised into teams of builders, accountants, salesmen and so on. A regular market in property was established and there were even rumours that a tunnel was under construction to the ladies' quarters. Access to the opposite sex was strictly forbidden under the general terms of residence which were naturally punitive. Mr Balls, however, was in great form. The man's hard green eyes had taken on a reddish glare and it would have taken a brave soul to stand against him. All the more villainous souls who might have kept him under control were at deeper levels of Hell and the purgatorial conditions on Level One rather enhanced his efforts as he braced himself to the challenges they offered with a certain relish.

It was this relish, this capacity for work and accomplishment, this power within the man that had attracted the Lady Hermione to him when both were in their vigorous prime upon Earth. For several years she had watched him with a certain longing composed in equal parts of sexual and of moral desire. It seemed to her that if his fine qualities could be harnessed to good ends he would be a man of a magnificence hard to equal. That this magnificence be subject to her will was possibly included in her desire but she was never to find out what might be, as circumstances were never propitious. Unspoken unfinished goings on remained between the two long after the vicissitudes of life had parted them from the same circles of events.

At last, word reached the Lord Satan of the creation of an alternative centre of power in the form of Stephen Balls. It threatened to get serious enough to unbalance the status quo. The main difficulty was not the man but the introduction of hope and enthusiasm. The great Beëlzebub shook his head with irritation and asked for an assessment of the feasibility of taking the culprit lower down the bottomless pit. But his activities did not qualify Stephen Balls for sterner punishment and, if they had, there would be no certainty that he would not continue with his trouble-making. It was decided to send him up to Heaven on one of the exchanges of souls scheduled now and then and Lord Satan smirked to think that his great rival would have to sort the problem out.

The Lord God accepted Stephen Balls after an interview in which Balls agreed to take a humble role and to keep his eyes lowered and his head bowed for an entire year. It was hard to say how long this might actually be when eternity has replaced time but, however long it should prove, Balls knew that there were times in business when you had to acknowledge a superior power and adopt a low profile with the eventual end of securing an advantageous position. A tiresomely meticulous record keeper pointed out that Mr. Balls had once refused to buy his little girl a pony as he did not care for the beasts and at once it was decreed to him that he should be in charge of sweeping the stable yard.

Thus it came about that the Lady Hermione, who had departed earthly life some time previously, caught sight of Stephen Balls with a straw between his clenched teeth and his head down to his work. She was strolling by the stables laughing and joking with a troop of attendant suspiciously male- looking angels. It had been noted in higher quarters for some time that she had too much leisure and was possibly of a sensual inclination. It had already been decided that something was to be done about this soon when the unexpected event took place that changed the situation forever.

None of this would have happened had there not been something of a history between these two from their time on Earth. Despite the difference in their original social status they had met by chance after Stephen Balls had built up a property empire and the Lady Hermione was indulging in renovations. They found themselves after the same desirable property in Brighton and a meeting had been arranged to negotiate the matter such that they would not raise the price by bidding against each other. Stephen Balls had been socially uncertain and the Lady H, startled by the attraction that she felt for his raw power, nevertheless expected to have her own way as was usual, due to her charm and beauty. A number of meetings amounting to unspoken dates followed, but in the clash of will passion had taken second place and remained unrealized. Stephen acquired the property and Hermione was impressed and piqued in equal measure.

Now there is a mechanism between souls whereby, should there be unfinished matters between them, they can occasionally recognise each other in the afterlife. It is an atavistic remnant of the passions of Earth deemed to have been eradicated but inclined to erupt unexpectedly from time to time. As Hermione passed to the closest point from Stephen she glanced into the yard. At the same time that her memory prompted recognition of those shoulders and that tightly curled hair he despite having undertaken to keep his eyes lowered and having been forbidden from looking onto the Heaven-dwellers, looked up for a moment. Their eyes met and they knew each other.

Although Lady Hermione hurried away and Stephen returned at once to his work there is no mistaking the tremors that occur in the ether when something of this kind happens. Personality is not to be invoked. It is not to be enjoyed nor even endured. It is an unseemly interruption of bliss amounting to a challenge to the superiority of that state. The result was that both their cases were listed once more for review.

At their subsequent meeting God remarked to Satan that passion was a devilish thing and ought to be so classified. Satan, who knew and valued the power of passion to disturb eternal bliss, was unyielding. Passion must remain classified as morally neutral and retain the ability arising from its outcomes to discern the better from the worse. It was clear to both that the play between the two humans would be a play between them also.

With a certain sense of humour not perhaps to be admitted to and a sense of justice that thrilled with potential for their rivalry, the reincarnation clause was invoked for Stephen Balls and the responsibility clause for the Lady Hermione. He was found upon adequate trial to have fitted in neither to Heaven nor to Hell and was ordered to be reborn forthwith into the human race for the further exercise of moral choice and in the hopes of a more definite outcome. She was promoted to the rank of Junior Guardian Angel where she would have a good deal less time on her hands. Amongst others she was given particular responsibility for the welfare and guidance of the soul of Stephen Balls as it embarked afresh upon human life. Mysterious are the ways of the gods and what happened next is another story.

―――ooOoo―――

Briony Kapoor grew up on Romney Marsh, was at school in Suffolk, and at University in Northumberland. After worldwide travel she owned an art gallery in Central London before settling for many years in India with her husband, a distinguished academic. As a widow, she returned to build her own house from where she is generally engaged in various projects.

THE BIKE

Lisamarie Lamb

The bike is still there, still chained to the lamp post, still waiting for her. *I* am still waiting for her. The difference, however, between me and the bike is that *I* know she isn't coming back. I've spent a year knowing that, dying a little each time I hear her name, each time I hear her voice in my head.

I'd bought her the bike for Christmas and she, like a child, the child she wanted still to be but couldn't because she was a grown up, a wife, a mother, a real person in the real world, had beamed and grinned and shrieked at it. At me. She had run her gloveless fingers across the handlebars and over the leather of the saddle, squeezing it slightly, glancing at me cheekily as she did it. Her feet were bare and she was standing on the patio in freezing December weather wearing nothing but a pair of pink checked pyjamas. I remember that so clearly. I remember her face, reddened by the chill wind. I remember her smile behind cracked lips. I remember her dark hair – nothing hair, she called it – dancing in the wind.

It wasn't nothing hair. There was nothing *nothing* about her. She was everything. And she loved that bike. And she loved me for giving her that bike. She loved it for a day. Just over. A few hours over. Since then it had been chained to the lamp post outside the library getting rained on and sunned on and sat on by strangers who didn't understand. I always chased them away, careful not to steer them into the road. But they shouldn't be touching it.

It was a good Christmas that year. Last year. A quiet Christmas. Just me and her and the kid. And the bike. I could see her keep looking at it, her eyes drawn towards it as we celebrated, as we ate and drank and played games and watched silly television programmes that we'd never watch at any other time of the year. Just a little flicker of her eyes, that was all. And it made me so happy. Who would have thought a thing like a bike would make a thirty-five year old woman so excited? But it did.

When we went to bed that night, tipsy and a little too noisy, she was still grinning. "Thank you," she said, and she kissed me on my red-tinged lips. I can still feel it, that kiss. I can still smell her nothing hair, the scent of almonds wafting up at me because she'd used the baby's shampoo instead of her own. Sometimes now I use that shampoo myself, but it's not the same. It isn't her.

The next morning she had a headache, we both did, but she still wanted to ride the bike. She couldn't wait any longer and I said I'd wait for her at home, have a lunch of cold meat and bubble and squeak and pickles – leftovers, but what else do you eat on Boxing Day? – ready for her when she got back. I gave her a quick peck on the forehead, a goodbye kiss, a goodbye forever kiss except I didn't know it, and watched her wobble down the path and onto the street. No helmet. I hadn't bought a helmet. Why hadn't I? Would she have worn one over her nothing hair? But then I didn't think about it, I turned back to the children and pulled them apart since they were arguing over some toy or other.

In the end it didn't matter about the helmet. It wasn't the bike that killed her. She reached the library. That's where she had chosen to go, she said she would pop her overdue books through the door and hope they would forgive her the fine, since it was

Christmas. She propped her bike, her wonderful new bike, up against the lamp post. She locked it. And she walked away from it.

She walked away from the bike and then she stopped walking. She stood, a pause, and her hand fluttered up to her face, up to her head, and then she fell. That's what the witnesses said. That's what they told me with their sad eyes and sorrowful voices. She walked, she stopped, she died. A brain aneurism. Thirty-five. A wife. A mother.

—ooOoo—

Lisamarie Lamb lives in Minster, Kent

TIME SHADOWS

Sue Peake

My Internet server front page said: *"You have one unread email."* Clicking through to my inbox I read, *"William@Forefathers.com."* Strange! Although I'd paid an expensive annual subscription fee to enable me to use *Forefathers.com* to research my family tree, for several months I hadn't actually visited the Website. Occasionally I had exchanged emails with a fellow member regarding my family tree during the time it had slowly grown from seed to sapling online, but that was it. When my searching for ancestral answers hit a brick wall, or, more accurately, The Great Wall of China, I had lost interest. A fascinating, but very frustrating, hobby!

In the short time I was delving, I thought I'd done quite well; finding my great-great-grandfather George's details, but there it had ended. I only knew, from his death certificate, that his father had been a William. Then came The Great Wall, and despite me dipping into every similar website that the computer unearthed for me, I couldn't find William's date or place of birth.

I did uncover other ancestors though – one as far back as the Sixteenth Century who had been hanged by the Crown for high treason, but this had hardly helped me Williamwise.

I clicked on the icon of a stern man wearing a ruff and up popped my email. *"I was born in 1765 in Shuttlebay, Essex, and died in 1830. My parents were Josiah and Frances. I was a mast-maker by trade. Your obedient servant, William."*

Was someone trying to be funny? As I'd registered my research interests on the net, it was quite possible that they'd been viewed and a comedian was pretending to help. Oh! ha! ha! I deleted the message.

When, over dinner, I told my husband, William – yes, another William – about it, he was mildly amused and that, I thought, was that.

Two weeks later, I received another email:

Why have you not put my details on our family tree? I thought you were interested in genealogy. I am most disappointed. I really hoped that my descendants would be more intelligent and persevering. Your humble servant, William

For goodness sake! This was getting beyond a joke. This time I tried a different tactic, namely, returning the email to its origin with a few impolite added words. It didn't work. The be-ruffed Elizabethan informed me that my message could not be delivered to an invalid address. I tried several more times without success, and then gave up. It was only a week before the next email came:

I really wish that you would come and see me, Abigail. My gravestone is at St. John's Church in Shuttlebay. It is only a small churchyard, so it will be simple to find me. Please come. I have not been visited for a long time. I am lonely here. Yours, William

I jabbed at the 'delete' button so hard, the laptop skittered across the table. Someone had a weird sense of humour. I didn't sleep well that night; 1 had nightmares of ghosts and ghouls with William cackling at me in the guise of a green phosphorescent blob on the church roof.

My husband gave me his opinion. 'Why don't you go to Shuttlebay? Your sister lives near there. You could visit her during the same trip. These emails might be someone's idea of a strange joke, but the facts in them could be true. You've got nothing to lose.'

The idea nagged at me for the next few days, and nights. I wasn't keen. It was a long drive, but I was due time off work, and perhaps my William was right. It was a very odd way of presenting data, but the information was not necessarily false.

I decided to go, but, to avoid ridicule, I wouldn't say anything to anyone, not even my sister, about my mission. Only my William would know. I'd even turn up at the hotel without a reservation. Normally, I liked planning ahead but I couldn't rid myself of the thought that someone was watching my every move. I'd rung the local tourist information office to be told, surprisingly, that there was a good hotel in the centre of Shuttlebay with Internet access in the rooms – very useful. In a small seaside town, out of season, it would hardly be fully booked.

It was a miserable day so William and I said goodbye indoors. Then, with a final distasteful look at the depressing grey sky and sea, I took a deep breath and stepped outside. Secrecy had become my obsession. Wearing a hood to cover my head, I slipped into my car, having placed my travel bag in the boot the previous evening. I had thought of wearing a mask too, but it would have blocked my view of the motorway.

By the time I got to Shuttlebay, I felt more relaxed. I'd had fun with my sister, whom I rarely saw, catching up and sharing news of our respective children. My Amelia was in advertising and sons George and Joseph were jointly running an antique shop. Her sons were still a big worry for her - regularly scrounging money and being mixed up in dodgy deals.

I had kept my smug thoughts that we had been more fortunate, to myself. When we were children, I had envied Jane for being the prettier and more popular one. Now, words could be grenades in our hands, exploding our fragile relationship.

It was approaching dusk by the time I got to St. John's Church, having checked in at my hotel first. I may have erased the emails from my computer but not from my memory - every word of them was haunting me.

With the square Norman church tower watching over its territory like a fat uncle, I wandered around the churchyard in the drizzle, getting lost on the gravel paths that all looked identical. It was a pretty place, especially with the cherry trees just in blossom.

I took a few photos with my digital camera. Some lichen-encrusted headstones had illegible words, others were half-crumbled, and I wondered if I was wasting my time. On the point of giving up, I finally saw it, right at the back. His grave was overgrown with long grasses and weeds, but the headstone was surprisingly clean. It depicted a simple cross with, at the base, this inscription

Sacred to the memory of William Delaware.
1765 – 1830.
Beloved husband of Abigail.
Father of Amelia, George and Joseph.
His memory never fadeth.

A chill went through me. Suddenly every ghostly graveyard cliché seemed real. The fact that my own name was shared by his wife, and that our children had the same names was, quite frankly, unnerving. I expected the sky to darken yet further and, with a loud clap of thunder, a white wraith to hover whilst huge worms slithered over the grave.

Nothing happened. Nothing at all. The birds continued singing; the trees rustled; I got wetter in the rain.

I wanted to run but told myself not to be silly. Instead I quickly snapped off a few pictures of the headstone and left. I took ten steps before my courage disappeared. Feeling that I was being watched and judged unworthy, I dashed to the car.

Back in my hotel room, I made myself a coffee and looked at the photos. All very pretty scenic shots of the church and trees but yes, of course, another cliché had popped up – none of the pictures of *the* grave had come out. Oh well, it was a new and complicated camera. In my haste, I'd probably pressed the wrong buttons.

Sleep came uneasily that night….

The next morning, feeling braver, I decided to re-visit the grave and try taking more photographs. I stopped at a garage en-route to fill the tank, snatching up a bouquet of carnations before paying. Sentimental to put flowers on the grave of an ancient ancestor? Probably, but in some silly way, it felt right.

It was a lovely sunny day, making me laugh at my fears of the previous evening as I carefully laid the flowers on the stone. Reaching for my camera, I realised that I'd left it at the hotel. How stupid, but never mind, I'd sketch the headstone. While I was doing this, the sensation of being observed came back strongly. In spite of the sun cheerily beaming down, I was spooked, and found myself nervously turning my head this way and that. The only human in sight was an elderly lady tending a fresh grave, seeming hunched and forlorn. Nevertheless, I decided it was time to return to the hotel. I'd be travelling home today.

I was expecting work to contact me, so, back in my room, I checked for any emails on my laptop before checking out. "Forefathers.com" had sent me another email from William.

'This time I'll get you.' I muttered, directing my anger towards the mysterious joker. 'There's no way you know that I'm here, and as soon as I get home, I'll change my email address.' Wearily, I read the message.

"Thank you, but I do not like carnations. William."

―――ooOoo―――

WAITING

Sue Peake

It was a Thursday, the first time my mother wore funeral clothes. Normally she dressed as brightly as a tropical bird, but today she wore a little dark hat with a discreet veil, and a black trouser suit. As a night shadow, she glided across the room, and sat on the chaise longue, like a black little Miss Muffet.

'Mum, what on earth are you wearing?'

She peered around, then hissed, 'It's a secret. Promise me, don't breathe a word.'

Humour her. 'I promise'.

'Your father, he won't live much longer.'

'What are you talking about?' In other words, what latest insect under Miss Muffet's bonnet?

'I've been told, Misty knows.'

Oh God, not Misty again. Misty the telephone psychic, into whose plastic ear my mother had sent hundreds of pounds. Must be careful what I say, when coping with mental illness.

'What does Misty know?'

'Within the year he'll be dead. I have to be prepared'. A serene smile.

I know she hates him, but this is ridiculous. Their marriage is a deep ocean where I fear to swim, silences thick as treacle, punctuated by screaming matches. Reason has flown out of our house on bats' wings.

Misty was the latest in an endless line of escapist fantasies, each one weirder than the last. Mum rang her daily, premium rate of course, and had long secretive conversations that ceased whenever I came near. Ironically, another frequent row was the cost of the phone bills.

Time passed, and this particular whim outlived (excuse the pun) the others. Mum spent yet more on Dad's credit cards, and wore a different funereal outfit virtually every day, from a store aptly named Black's. The most recent hat sprouted a clump of black ostrich feathers. Dad, if he even noticed or cared, made no comments on her novel attire.

She spoke more quietly, and despite her initial secrecy, had begun hinting to friends about her impending widowhood. Father she watched like a hawk. The rows decreased, silences stretched longer than ever, but she was waiting now. If he complained of a headache, she wondered to me if it was a brain tumour, and if indigestion was the sign of an impending heart attack. When he was late home from work, she speculated on car crashes. Even I was getting paranoid, though I myself was waiting – to have saved up enough for a deposit on a flat … and be rid of them both.

The deadline (sorry!) was the 11th of January. Christmas was meagre – no point, she said, I can splash out when I get the insurance money; why buy him an expensive present since he won't be around to enjoy it. She began writing lists of funeral directors, and debated on what type of cheap wood was cheapest for the coffin.

Rita over the road, another Misty fan, was let into the secret. She and Mum planned a month in a villa in Lanzarote in February.

Mum's patience was wearing thin by early January. I heard her speak to Misty, and remark that he seemed fit and well, and surely she'd waited long enough. She hovered over her bureau with bundles of insurance documents in her hand, which she hastily shoved in a drawer when she heard me coming. I was out as much as possible, stressed with the tension of time pulled as taut as a bow, living with the obsession of a non-grieving widow-to-be.

The 11th of January was freezing. Snow covered our lawn for the first time, and now it was likely that Dad would slip on the ice, fall in the river, or skid in the car. At 12.01 on 12th January, Dad's snores filled our home. Mum stormed into my
Bedroom, screeching: "He's still alive! He's still alive! I rang Misty, and the phone's dead. Unlike Dad, I thought. "The number's unobtainable. I'm going to Rita's".

'Mum, you can't go at this time of night. Go in the morning!'

The slamming of the front door was the only answer, followed by a scream and the squeal of brakes. I dashed out into the road, where Mum lay in a pool of melting ice, the street lamp turning her blood to sepia. Over and over, the driver kept muttering, "She's dead; she just ran out, I couldn't stop".

I looked at my watch. Dad would need to go to Black's in the morning.

—ooOoo—

Sue Peake enjoys writing poetry and also pens personalised poems for clients who request these on any topic from birth to death. She loves travel, photography and cats.

CENTRING THE OLIVES

Michele Sheldon

Huxley Harrison thought he would be stuck on olives forever. He had stood for seven hours a day, for six months placing one slippery black olive onto the centre of each pizza as they sped by on the conveyor belt. This was not how his life was meant to be. Huxley used to have plans. He used to have ambition. Huxley also used to love olives. He used to savour plain black or green, stuffed or marinated, especially those filled with chillies. But now he detested them. He couldn't bear to look at their waxy rubber coats. And the thought of even placing one near his mouth filled him with dread. However, he did have a certain begrudging respect for them. After all, the olive was King Harry's unique selling point.

Huxley also used to hate his fellow workers for they had snubbed any attempts at conversation during lunch and tea breaks and shunned him on the production line. He had wanted nothing more than to leave King Harry's far behind. But he was trapped by £10,000 of debt accrued from a modern history degree and a year of applying for 456 jobs in the media. He'd had three interviews but received no job offers except for internships on *Paint Removal Monthly* and its sister title, *Cornice Restoration*. Both roles were unpaid and in London, over two hours away by train. Unlike some of his friends' parents, his were unwilling to help anyone but themselves. His father had left long ago and his mother, although physically in the family home, drank herself absent most days.

So during his induction day at King Harry's, Huxley could do nothing more than bite his tongue as Audrey, the supervisor, a wiry woman in her 30s with buck teeth, told him how lucky he was to get the job as a factory operative.

'Congratulations Huxley! You beat 203 applicants,' she said. 'It was a close call between you and another young man.' Audrey leant towards him conspiratorially. 'But he had a few personal hygiene problems,' she said, crinkling her nose in disgust. 'Do you have high hygiene standards, Huxley?'

Huxley was taken aback by the question. 'Of course I do,' he said, surreptitiously sniffing his armpits as she turned away to pass him his mug of tea. He took a sip of the sweet, sickly mixture and his heart sank as he thought about how awful the 201 other applicants must have been. Getting the job had initially cheered Huxley up. He had been looking forward to earning some money and feeling some pride in going to work every day. But with Audrey's revelation each drop of happiness was rapidly dissolving.

'He also had a rotten attitude towards pizzas and ideas above his station. Do you have ideas above your station, Huxley?' said Audrey. 'Modern history wasn't it?' she added suddenly, making Huxley jump in his chair.

'Yes,' muttered Huxley.

'Very interesting I'm sure for a hobby but not very practical in the world of pizzas,' said Audrey, patting his knee, not waiting for him to answer. 'We don't need to know the key dates of the Second World War or why Hitler invaded Poland while we're making a nice pepperoni pizza for little Bobby's birthday party. It's all part of our APE.'

'Sorry?' said Huxley suddenly thrown by the introduction of primates into the conversation.

'APE! It's in your induction manual, Huxley. It stands for Ace Pizza Experience. It's what we all strive for here at King Harry's.'

'Oh,' said Huxley, feeling as though Audrey may as well have smashed a sledgehammer down on his head and mashed his brain.

'Our pizzas lift people's spirits, Huxley. That's all people really want during a recession – a cheap yummy King Harry's Pizza. It helps to take their minds off their money worries and to see the positive things in life. This other chap thought that pizzas were below him. He had a degree in geography and reckoned he could name every country we source our ingredients from. A bit of a smart Alec, although not so clever at finding his way around the personal hygiene products in Boots,' smiled Audrey insincerely.

Huxley nodded his head in agreement, noting that the last smidgen of glee had finally left him. He watched Audrey stare wistfully at the production line while crunching on her ginger nut and hoped this marked the end of Audrey's tirade against modern history.

'You'll never get on with an attitude like that at King Harry's! That's not how I became supervisor, I can tell you that for nothing!' said Audrey sweeping away the crumbs from the corners of her mouth with her pointy, lizard-like tongue.

After they'd finished their mugs of tea, Audrey showed him around the huge cavernous factory of shiny metal fixtures and fittings and bright white walls covered in signs telling people not to smoke, run or talk. Huxley had always been curious about the factory. Nearly everyone in the town had a mum, dad, brother, sister, uncle, aunt, cousin or friend who worked at King Harry's. And everyone had a freezer packed full of King Harry pizzas whether they liked them or not. Huxley was struck by the loyalty that King Harry's inspired among the workforce. He'd never heard a bad word about the factory which dominated the pretty town and harbour, sitting on the hillside like an ugly scar. But Huxley always thought there was something malevolent about the factory, the way it consumed most of the town's working population in its 24-hour-a-day production, the smell of pizza permeating the town, messing with people's appetites. What was also odd was how the sea mist's icy fingers chose to clasp onto the factory buildings, leaving nearby streets mist-free and bathed in sunshine, as if it were in league with King Harry to hide its dark secrets from prying eyes. Huxley patiently observed the factory operatives expertly sprinkling grated cheese on top of the pizzas and pasting tomato sauce on pale doughy bases.

'It's an art form isn't it Huxley?' said Audrey as they both stared in admiration at the mysterious gloved hands tossing pizza bases through a small square window from the bakery onto the production line. 'You can work your way up to the bakery but first we'll be starting you off on the olive station,' said Audrey, taking him to the end of the production line where a squat middle-aged man was placing an olive in the centre of each pizza as they sped past.

The man dipped a pudgy hand into the huge vat of black olives standing before him and deftly grabbed a handful. His fat fingers were surprisingly agile as they delicately placed an olive in the centre of each pizza. After five minutes, Huxley was allowed to take over the task but found himself unable to keep up with the speed of the conveyor belt and several pizzas whizzed by olive-less. The production line quickly stopped and everyone turned to look at Huxley.

Audrey came rushing over. 'It's okay Huxley! We'll keep it slower this morning. By this afternoon, you'll have the hang of it,' said Audrey.

Huxley blushed. He felt useless and pathetic. He couldn't even put an olive on a pizza properly. No wonder no-one had wanted to employ him, thought Huxley. But within ten minutes, Huxley had finally got the hang of centring olives and Audrey gave the nod for the production line to speed up.

Huxley had assumed that the operatives would be moved around from one task to another regularly to avoid boredom. He had also assumed that his training would last one day at the most. But on the second day, Huxley had still not been assigned to any other task other than placing an olive in the middle of a pizza. He spent his time enviously watching the other operatives switch from cheese sprinkling to tomato pasting, from pepperoni placing to pineapple chunk arranging. Huxley was itching to get his hands into the cheese and feel it dropping from his fingers onto the never ending circle of pizzas. At night, he even began dreaming about delicately pasting on a luxurious bed of tomato sauce for slices of ham and pineapple, showering the production line with grated cheese and kneading the doughy bases without any gloves on.

At the end of his third day, he'd put his extended olive duty down to an impromptu visit by Fatcat Supermarkets who were doing a spot check on the production of their new range aimed at young girls, Princess Pizzas. Huxley assumed that Audrey had wanted to keep the new boy on a simple task so that he wouldn't mess up the production line during their visit. Princess Pizzas were regular sized pizzas covered in tomato sauce, with an olive, of course, but one that had been bleached then dyed pink. The whole pizza was finished off with a sprinkling of edible gold and silver glitter. After being wrapped in plastic, the pizzas were then inserted into pink boxes decorated with pictures of a benevolent King Harry and his beautiful flaxen-haired daughter, Princess Margareta. Huxley understood. He didn't want to ruin Audrey's perfect production line either. So, he stood all day, apart from his half an hour lunch break and his two ten minute tea breaks, placing his olives slap bang in the centre of each pizza that flew past.

On day four, he put his enforced olive centring down to an oversight by Audrey after all the excitement of the Princess Pizzas. But by day five it suddenly dawned on Huxley that he was still in training. Audrey had quite clearly left him there because he was not up to doing any other pizza-making related tasks. Huxley desperately wanted to find out what was going on. So, at morning tea break he plucked up the courage to ask a kindly looking lady in her 60s, who had once smiled at him in the canteen. But as soon as he approached she scuttled into the toilets. Huxley was initially stunned by her reaction and then felt a rage burn through him. He waited for her to come out.

'Why am I always on olives?' he demanded.

'You're the new olive boy,' she whispered as if that were all the answer he needed.

'What do you mean, the new olive boy?' asked Huxley desperately. All sorts of hideous situations crept into his mind. Did this mean he would be the olive boy forever? That this was all he would ever achieve? And what happened to the old olive boy? Had King Harry executed him for not centring the olives?

'Shhh! Keep your voice down, boy! They watch and hear everything. You're never alone at King Harry's!'

Huxley followed her vacant blue eyes around the room where they flickered up to the ceiling. Four cameras zoomed down on them. Huxley stormed over to Audrey's office, knocking crossly at the door.

'What can I do for you Huxley?' asked Audrey, not bothering to look up at him.

'I'd like to do something other than olives please.'

'Do you want this job Huxley? Because, as I said, there are hundreds out there who'd bite your hand off for a job here,' she said finally looking up.

'Well, yes,' swallowed Huxley, remembering all the unopened and unpaid bills littering the kitchen table at home.

'Well, let's not run before we've learnt to walk then, Huxley.'

'But it's just putting olives on a pizza.'

'Oh is it now!' said Audrey, standing up from her chair sharply and marching towards Huxley. 'That's exactly what he said.'

'Who said?'

'Your predecessor, the old olive boy.'

'What happened to him?'

'He couldn't centre.'

'What do you mean?'

'He kept missing!'

'How can you not centre!' said Huxley to himself.

'Exactly! I like your attitude Huxley.' Audrey said as she glanced at her watch. 'Tea break over. Back to work now, Huxley. You show us how you can centre those olives boy!'

But after two weeks of centring olives, Huxley now understood why the old olive boy hadn't been able to centre. His fingers were refusing to do what he told them. They were aching from being in the same position day in day out. At night he even bathed them in a bowl of hot water to ease the muscle cramps. They wanted to be stretched. They were threatening to go on strike. And on day 14 Huxley gave in to their demands. He looked around furtively and then placed two olives just off centre, then another three and four, until the pizzas were decorated with five olives spread in a cross. Someone, somewhere would get a big olive surprise, smiled Huxley to himself. He felt his heart bursting with joy at the thought that his olive formation was probably groundbreaking, that it had probably never been attempted at King Harry's before. He didn't care if he got into trouble. He felt free for the first time in weeks. Then a few moments later, the production line came to an abrupt halt and everyone looked across at Huxley accusingly.

'I don't need to tell an intelligent young man like you, Huxley, that the olive is an integral part of the ace pizza experience,' said Audrey who had escorted him into her office for his own safety. 'We don't like people messing with our magic formula, Huxley! And they,' she said, gesturing to the workers standing around the still production line glaring in at the office, 'don't like being messed around. The olive is why Fatcat Supermarkets buy our pizzas for 50 pence each and are able to sell them to their customers for £4.99. An olive screams quality, Huxley. It brings a bit of class into the little people's lives. It's like finding a Belgian praline in a cheap box of fruit centres. People do not want to see five olives on their pizzas. With one olive, they think they're lucky. If we give them five, they will think: why not six or seven? Comprendo?'

'Yes,' muttered Huxley, his heart sinking further than he ever thought possible.

'All you need to remember is that the olive is King Harry's signature. And King Harry is like a god round here. You don't want to anger a god, do you, Huxley?' said Audrey who was standing so close to Huxley that he could smell her tea breath.

'No! Of course not,' said Huxley, feeling suddenly humbled.

'Well then, centre the olives Huxley and King Harry may find it in his heart to forgive you. But first of all what do you say to King Harry?'

'Sorry,' mumbled Huxley feeling like a small child again.

'Say it like you mean it,' shouted Audrey.

'I'm sorry, King Harry!' said Huxley.

'Go APE, Huxley! I know you've got it in you,' said Audrey, patting him on his back.

Huxley resisted the urge to push Audrey away and tell her where he'd like to stick her precious pizzas. He had a brain. He had ambition. He wanted a proper job where he could shine. But he remembered the final reminder for the gas bill that his mother still hadn't paid. Huxley forced himself to smile. 'But...but when can I do something else, like cheese sprinkling?'

'Your time will come. King Harry will know when you're ready.'

Six months later when Huxley arrived for work one morning, Audrey and all the operatives were gathered in the locker room. As he pushed open the door, they suddenly erupted into cheers and applause. Some were even punching the air with joy.

'Congratulations Huxley!' said Audrey, thrusting a pizza-shaped piece of paper at him.

'You've done us proud! We're moving you onto cheese!'

Huxley felt himself blush at the attention. He looked down at the piece of paper in his shaky hands. It was a certificate. It read:

You've gone APE on the Olive Station. Well done! It had even been signed by King Harry himself with his huge, sloping, majestic signature.

'If you make a good job of cheese, the world is your oyster, Huxley! Come here!' Audrey grabbed Huxley and squeezed him tightly. 'I knew you had it in you, Huxley!' she added.

Huxley tried to smile. King Harry may be watching. Anyway, why shouldn't he be pleased with himself, thought Huxley. He wasn't so useless after all. He felt a glow of satisfaction spread through him and grinned at the cameras. Then he suddenly felt troubled. Would he be up to the job? His fingers had eventually knuckled down to some hard work after their rebellion but would they be able rise to the challenge and be flexible enough to sprinkle cheese? Doubts crashed in on Huxley and he felt faint. All the operatives filed past him, each and every one of them had snubbed him as the new olive boy, but now stopped to shake his hand and offer words of congratulations.

'You sit for a few minutes, Huxley. It's a lot to take in. Then I'll get you acquainted with the grated cheese,' said Audrey.

'But who's going to do the olives?' asked Huxley panicking.

'Don't worry,' said Audrey patting his head. 'We have a new olive girl.'

A few minutes later, Huxley shook with joy as he donned his plastic gloves and plunged his hands into a huge tub of the grated cheese, feeling its coldness running between his fingers. He closed his eyes in ecstasy.

'Feels good, doesn't it Huxley?' Audrey whispered.

Huxley smiled and glanced over at the olive station. The new olive girl was hard at work. She was young, maybe just 18. Her white overalls hung off her bony frame, her harsh profile partially hidden by the King Harry's regulation cap. Huxley felt a sudden stab of pity as he watched her concentrating on centring each olive, and wondered if the thought of being stuck on olives forever had crossed her mind yet.

But he couldn't spare the time to worry about the new girl. He had bigger fish to fry. Huxley had to focus on scooping out the exact amount of cheese required by King Harry for each pizza. That afternoon, just as he was feeling confident in his sprinkling abilities, the production line suddenly stopped. Everyone, including Huxley, immediately knew where the fault lay. They stared across at the new olive girl who was hunched over the conveyor belt, sobbing. She had somehow managed to knock over the vat of olives. They were now scattered over the belt and floor like mini-cockroaches. Huxley tutted. At this rate he would never get onto the tomato sauce station.

—ooOoo—

THE MANTELPIECE

Michele Sheldon

I'd been sent to the house as a punishment. My boss had decided that the cracked mantelpiece lying at my feet that Friday morning was my fault, even though I'd sworn it had been one very solid piece of marble when I'd fork-lifted it into the elevator. However, as the words left me, I realised blaming the ancient, jerky lift made me sound guilty. Mr Tweed told me that antiques had a habit of breaking or spontaneously combusting in my presence and to get out of his sight.

'I've got a job for you, Ben. You're just pricing, so there's no need for excessive handling, understand?'

'Monday then,' I said as I picked up my coat to leave.

'Monday? Not after this! You're going now and will spend the whole weekend there until you've finished."

'Oh, but I've got plans...'

'And I had plans for this £2,000 mantelpiece,' he interrupted, tracing the jagged crack with his thumb. 'See if you can absolve yourself and find me something interesting.'

He took a grubby, crumbled piece of paper out of his jacket pocket and thrust it at me.

'Even you can't possibly miss it.'

Deeply buried childhood memories flooded back as I read the address. East Cliff House was a well-known landmark on account of its size, cliff top location and giant conker tree. My cousin, Paul, had lived on the estate half a mile away and one day he'd dared me to climb over the high iron gates to reach the fresh conkers still dressed in their spiky green jackets. I remembered the thud and terror of landing on the wrong side of the gates, and Paul's urgent pleas for me to hurry as the front door opened and two ghostly, grey-haired figures appeared. I'd scrambled back over and we'd run and run until our lungs were fit for bursting.

'Off you go then,' said Mr Tweed.

I'd quickly tried to think of an excuse. My sister had invited me over that weekend and I'd been looking forward to having company now that Katie had left.

'But...there won't be anyone there?' I said.

After all, weekend work for the legal profession was a big no no. They kept strict working hours.

'The solicitor's expecting you.'

'On a Saturday?'

'The estate's been in probate for three years. They're keen to get it wrapped up.'

'On a Saturday?'

'Just get on with it, Ben.'

As I walked to my van, I vaguely recalled Katie telling me of a news report she'd seen about the mansion. The elderly lady who lived there had died leaving an estate worth millions and the solicitors were trying to trace relatives. But there was something dodgy, Katie had said; something about a fake name. I wished then that I'd been a better listener. In fact, being *a rubbish listener* was number two in the long list of my failings that Katie had outlined in her goodbye letter. I turned on the engine, feeling a sense of dread about being surrounded by the mysterious lady's belongings. When I first started the job, I used to love poking around strangers' houses, building up an image of what kind of person had lived there and, of course, there was always the chance that I'd find some treasure. And I did. In my first year I stumbled across a painting by a 1920s artist which sold for £7,000, and last year, a rare collection of creepy German dolls that fetched nearly £10,000. I nearly always found something of high value which is why Mr Tweed hadn't sacked me. Yet. However, the last few visits I'd felt like an intruder, rifling through their wardrobes, drawers, filing cabinets, as if picking their bones like a vulture. Now that Katie had gone, I worried whether there would be anyone to sort out my old junk when I died, or whether it would be left to some depressed stranger like me.

As I turned off the main coastal road down the bumpy single track, the huge conker tree came into view. It partially blocked the handsome Edwardian house which still looked as forbidding, though slightly less large than I remembered. Now the gates stood open and welcoming, although thistles, nettles and other mean plants had taken over most of the front lawn. I expected to be met by some fusty old solicitor. But when I pulled up, an attractive dark-haired woman in her late 20s, got out of her car and greeted me with a smile.

'You do know that Raymond and Sons have already priced the more valuable items,' she said.

'Oh, really,' I said, trying to hide my disappointment.

Raymondo was our biggest rival. A few years ago, we would have been given the pick of the furniture. Mr Tweed used to call Raymondo and his ilk the bottom feeders of house clearance, but after the fire incident, it was us who were now very much the flounders.

'Well, I'm sure I'll find something. After all these years, you have a knack for it.'

'Oh, Mr Tweed told me he was sending his *junior* assistant,' she said.

I could feel a blush spreading from my throat and was relieved when she looked away and fished around in her handbag before bringing out a small bunch of keys, handing them to me.

'You're not coming in?'

'Oh, no need. It's been in our care for the last three years since the old lady, Florence Sobell, died. Don't worry. The water and electricity are working. She left us enough money to maintain everything.'

I looked at the front garden and pulled a face.

'Well, we had to prioritise and get the roof repaired. The money's just running out. Let's just say it's taken a lot longer to deal with than anyone expected, what with not being able to find a birth certificate for Florence.'

'Yes, I heard all about it,' I lied, looking up at the inky black windows wondering what secrets they were hiding. 'What about her husband?'

'Jack? He died five years ago. His affairs were very straightforward. It's just Florence who's the mystery.'

At first sight the house looked as if it had been kept in good order. Often I come across houses belonging to the aged in states that would do Miss Faversham proud. I didn't blame the old folks. My nan was the same. I was always getting out the Hoover when I visited, sucking up cobwebs in corners. It's their eyes. But the cleaners here? They had no excuse.

And they knew the dead would never complain. Huge dust balls clung to the skirting boards and spindly-legged spiders hung from the high ceilings. My eyes began to water and I sneezed several times as I scouted around the rooms, Raymondo's handiwork becoming ever more apparent. He'd claimed any piece of furniture of potential value, from a lovely Victorian card table, to a rather worn chaise longue with his annoying red and green stickers. My mood didn't improve when I walked into the kitchen, opened up the kitchen cupboard and pulled out a 1950s Conran dinner set decorated in Raymondo stickers. After checking all the cupboards, I found several cups and glasses that we could sell as vintage for a few quid. Then in the cupboard under the sink, I discovered a bottle of Australian wine. I recognised the label. It was cheap and easily replaceable, I reasoned, as I grabbed it and took it upstairs for company.

The light was fading fast as I climbed the wide elegant staircase. When I reached the landing, I hesitated momentarily, wondering which room to explore first. All the doors were shut, apart from one at the end of the hallway, which stood slightly ajar as if inviting me in. I gently kicked it open and gasped as the sunset streamed in through the double glass doors, bathing everything in an orange glow. A beautiful mahogany 1930s double bed lay next to me, right opposite the glass doors that led out onto a large balcony.

'Bloody Raymondo,' I said, surveying the rest of the fixtures and fittings. The only items he hadn't bagsied were the numerous photos on the mantelpiece. I fumbled around for the keys, opened up the balcony doors and sank down into a damp wicker chair. The sea was calm and striped with rich blue tones that grew silvery as the sun dipped over the horizon. Katie would have loved it here. I flipped open my mobile, then took a few swigs before filling my glass up. My finger hovered over her number until I remembered she'd told me to stop ringing her. I guzzled down the rest of the wine and refilled my glass before lighting a cigarette. At least there would be no fire hazard out here, I thought, flicking my ash into an empty plant pot. It wasn't my fault that the stupid cigarette had tumbled off Mrs Manton's mantelpiece and fallen into a wastepaper bin containing several unwanted Jackie Collins' paperbacks. And it wasn't my fault that the temperamental fork lift truck had released the mantelpiece prematurely.

    I drained my glass as the dark skies consumed the last of the sun's rays. I then stood, wobbling slightly, worried that Tweedie would turn up unexpectedly. It was the sort of thing he liked doing when you were in his bad books. Back inside, I walked towards the mantelpiece to take a closer look at the photos. As I drew closer, I realised they only ever showed two people, presumably Jack and Florence. However, what struck me was that the couple never appeared in a photograph together. I peered at one of Florence, perhaps in her 30s, dressed in a 1960s red trouser suit, smiling into the camera. Except it wasn't a proper smile because her big brown eyes weren't all screwed up in the corners. They looked frightened of something that was beyond the camera, her secret, perhaps. Other photos showed her posing stiffly in front of the Eiffel Tower and the Corcovado, her eyes always hidden by a pair of large sunglasses. I assumed the photographer had been Jack as he was similarly photographed outside the Coliseum and on a sweeping golden beach. The only recent photo of Florence showed her in the garden, the sea and white cliffs in the background, wearing the same guarded smile. The wind had caught her hair, making it ridiculously bouffant. She looked fragile as if held together by glue, and I imagined a sudden gust lifting her up like a feather and sweeping her away across the Channel. Jack on the other hand seemed to get more handsome as he aged. Geeky and skinny when younger, his greyness made him look distinguished and worldly.

I leant down and peered at the photo.

'Who are you, Flo?' I whispered into the silence just as my mobile rang.

The shock of its loud ring made me stumble into the mantelpiece and I watched helplessly as several photos crashed to the floor.

'You idiot, Ben,' I cursed and scrambled to my knees, quickly assessing the damage.

Luckily, none of the glass or frames had broken. However, the back had come off the largest, showing a head shot of Jack, in his late 30s or 40s, grinning at the photographer and now me. As I turned it over carefully, I noticed a piece of yellowed paper was sticking out. I eased it out, thinking it was part of the tatty backing, when I recognised the distinctive lettering. It was a birth certificate. I opened it up and read, *Iris Muriel Sobell, born 1928* in neat black ink. Folded inside was a small black and white photo showing a smartly dressed middle-aged couple, straight-backed and proud, standing in front of two teenagers, the boy slightly older than the girl. The teenagers' heads were tilted towards one another and they smiled widely at the photographer as if sharing a joke. I turned over the photo and squinted at the faded brown stamp advertising the photographers, *Baron Studios, Mayfair*. Right at the bottom in spidery handwriting someone, presumably the photographer's assistant, had written: *Mr and Mrs Sobell with son, Jack and daughter, Iris, 1942.* I turned over the photo and studied the girl's big brown eyes, and then the photo of Florence in her trouser suit.

With shaky hands, I took my mobile out from my pocket and dialled the missed call number .Tweedie answered immediately.

'I think I've found something interesting.'

—ooOoo—

Michele Sheldon is a journalist who writes mostly about health. She moved to Folkestone from London with her partner and three children just before the 2007 earthquake shook the town. She likes to spend time in a parallel world inhabited by shipwrecked Amazonian lab monkeys, who live on a paradise island in the Channel created by the earthquake.

STIFF UPPER LIP: AN ENGLISH EDUCATION

Nick Spurrier

Visiting London in the 1950s was always a great excitement for us all. Once, almost as soon as we arrived, my father took me from Brown's Hotel between Dover and Albemarle Streets down to Green Park tube station, along one stop to Piccadilly Circus and then up to the bright neon flashing lights, the theatres and traffic, his boyish enthusiasm almost equalling mine in a different world to the small Shropshire village where he was the local doctor. But I also remember a less frivolous visit to the Cavalry Club at the other end of Piccadilly near Hyde Park Corner.

A silent brown coloured place, in contrast to Piccadilly Circus, with large arm chairs occupied, it seemed, by mainly older retired soldiers and a cloakroom that had nail brushes screwed to the side of the basins for the aid of those who had lost an arm, it would later become a familiar building. I would meet my father there for a drink or a meal when he came to London on his own and once be entertained at the bar by a general who swore furiously and without inhibition in the all male atmosphere. But at least one purpose of our first visit was to see a famous painting by John Charles Dollman of "Titus" Oates who sacrificed his life on the return from the South Pole in 1912. Entitled "A Very Gallant Gentleman", it shows the cavalry officer, walking to his death in the blizzard, bent against the wind, so that Captain Scott and his companions might have a better chance of survival.

Self-sacrifice was at the heart of Rudyard Kipling's poem "Gunga Din", a favourite of my father's, in which an Indian water carrier loses his life saving a British soldier, closing with the words

'You're a better man than I am, Gunga Din!' Another poem by Kipling was displayed in the downstairs lavatory at home, almost as if, while seated there, we might, with prolonged exposure, absorb its sentiments. 'If' is full of exhortations on how to live, ending 'you'll be a man, my son!'

The painting and the poems were lessons for living as were many of the stories my father told. One that he may only have told once but I felt it was dozens of times possibly sums up his idea of correct behaviour: A Spartan boy had a pet fox against all the rules of his school. While playing with it one day a master approached and, in fear of punishment, the boy hid it under his coat, where as he talked to the master, it bit into and gnawed at his chest. The pain, my father said, was terrible, but not once did the boy cry out or even betray the agony he was enduring on his face.

This endurance of pain and the necessity to hide emotion – being a 'man' – lay at the centre of my father's philosophy of life. He revelled in the story of the extraction of his tonsils at the age of 11 with a pair of scissors and without anaesthetic, though possibly this was common practice at the start of the twentieth century. And he also believed in toughening himself up with the self-infliction of pain, hitting the back of his hand with a metal spiked clothes brush then whirling his arm round until droplets of blood appeared.

Restraint of emotion in public also extended to those closer to him. He had an abhorrence of handholding amongst older couples and a reluctance to indulge in prolonged leave taking, his first wife complaining that when he left on a train for the Second World War he held back from hugging and kissing her. But these rather harsh rules for living and lack of public affection contrasted with the attention he gave his patients, to whose emotional as well as physical problems he always had a kind and understanding approach, engendering great loyalty.

He also loved animals, which were a joyous part of our childhood, with up to five cats, tortoises, a much adored though short-lived dachshund, Chinese geese and a pet hen, Biddy, the sole survivor of a flock. My mother despaired of my father's habit of bringing home stray creatures he had encountered, especially hedgehogs, and keeping them for a time in the house. He had a horror of cruelty to animals and, though he had hunted foxes regularly in the nineteen thirties, and once even otters, he turned against it later in life, occasionally criticising gamekeepers and North Shropshire hunt officials he met in local pubs. Once, on a drive back from Wales, he was appalled to find a small bird embedded in the front fender of the car and found it difficult to forgive himself when our oldest cat drowned trying to drink from the swimming pool because he had not left out milk or water.

Saying goodbye to my pet animals was one of my rituals before our thrice yearly journey back to boarding school to which my brother and I had been despatched, like the children of most middle class families who could afford it, at the age of seven or eight. I can still remember the dread that accompanied our car rides back to Ruyton IX Towns about a dozen miles from our home in Grinshill, the theme tune of Billy Bunter of Greyfriars, a programme that always seemed to be on the television just before we left, still lingering in my mind.

For some reason we started at Packwood Haugh in the summer rather than the more normal Michaelmas or autumn term. We were the only two new boys and of course there were no hugs, kisses or tearful farewells. If I cried it would have been, probably like many others, in bed at night, stifling my sobs in the sheets. But I vividly remember an exception to this in my second term, watching a new boy wracked with sobbing, tears streaming down his face as he played frenetically with a then popular toy – potato man. And about a year later I recall another boy really letting the side down when his parents arrived for a visit. He rushed at them, throwing his arms around his mother's waist and clung on as some of us looked on in astonishment at this totally un-English behaviour as did his father, an upright and eminent Queen's Counsel, who made a desperate attempt to distance himself from the appalling spectacle.

Visits of parents to the school and home exeats during the term were one of the few changes that the new headmaster, Edward Pease-Watkin, made to the school. Early morning cold baths and beating as a punishment remained, both of course required to be taken without flinching. And though he did introduce science into the curriculum, classics remained the core with history following on a close second. Geography lessons frequently involved the display of a huge canvas backed map, resplendent with large areas of pink denoting the British Empire that still included India, though recently independent. Of the films I remember seeing at school, 'Where No Vultures Fly' portrayed the British presence in Africa as a force for nothing but good and 'The Dam Busters' showed that we had won the war almost single handed. The Americans possibly helped a bit but the Russians might not have existed. For us, England was still the greatest country in the world. After all, hadn't a British-led expedition just conquered Everest?

The Library boasted a complete collection of the works of G.A.Henty – stories of empire and war, celebrating Victorian values and the English public school virtues of 'pluck' and 'toughness'. My father grew up at the height of the British Empire and, in 1918, with other officer cadets at the Royal Military Academy, Woolwich, and greatly resented missing action in the First World War. Like his two brothers he was a great sportsman, playing golf, swimming, and becoming a good amateur jockey. But above all he was a good boxer, winning in 1919 the Lightweight competition of the Amateur championships in what The Times sports correspondent called "a close and gruelling fight". He continued boxing, winning further medals and cups, but there is a feeling that he was somehow punishing himself. In a letter to his mother in 1936, while training to be a doctor at St Mary's Hospital, he wrote 'I was boxing again last night but feel I must give it up because I find myself dreading it for days beforehand, as though the simple fact that I don't like it ought not to be sufficient to make me give it up.'

It was inevitable that we would be expected to box, even though I was hopelessly short sighted and underweight, and my brother susceptible to nose bleeds. An old army colleague of my father, Edward Sebastian Burke Gallfry, wrote in a letter, after recounting his own son's 'most bloody encounter as a heavyweight against a corporal of his own regiment, whom he managed to overcome', 'I have no doubt you are already training your two youngsters as lightweights of the future.' But I dreaded the boxing that my father insisted we do at Packwood Haugh right from the start. However, useless as I was, there were signs that my father's exhortations had hit home and that a stiff upper lip was emerging, as a school report shows: 'His boxing has been something of a disappointment because he still seems unable to box with his mouth shut and this in turn causes him to lean backwards to avoid being hit in his mouth. He is amazingly brave however in the way in which he takes all these blows.'

Other reports are full of accounts of my lack of success but always accompanied by comments on my ability to take punishment without complaint: 'He never gave up, and kept going the whole time', and accounts of plucky but obviously pathetic performances. My worst experience was an enforced match against a boy with whom I had been discovered fighting. As I stood there in the 'textbook' defensive posture, left fist forward and right fist next to my chin, he charged at me ignoring all the rules, head bent forward both fists flying, and pounded me like a demented robot. It was the most humiliating experience of my short boxing career and I have no recollection of any more bouts. I expect my father quietly allowed me to drop it as it sadly dawned on him that I would never be a great sportsman.

If Pease-Watkin as a young Headmaster did make attempts to change Packwood, which was on the whole a happy school, Shrewsbury School, on the cusp of the sixties had changed little since the 1920s when the Headmaster, J.M. Petersen, had been the head boy, captain of the cricket eleven, captain of fives and a member of the football eleven. Following a similar successful career in both the sports and academic spheres at Oxford, he became an assistant master at Eton, returning to Shrewsbury to become headmaster in 1950. He probably felt that what had been a successful school for him as a young man was fine as it was.

So all the arcane privileges and rules developed and refined since the time of Samuel Butler's revival of the school's fortunes in the early nineteenth century remained, upheld and enforced by senior boys. Bullying was virtually legitimised by the institution of douling, more usually called fagging at other public schools, whereby the younger boys acted as semi-servants to the older ones. One duty was to spit and polish the boots of your study monitor for the weekly parade of the Combined Cadet Force, formerly called the Officer Training Corps, presumably established with the expectation that, should the country ever go to war again, we would be the backbone of the British army. Each year there was field day, normally resulting in groups of us being dumped in the middle of the countryside and having to make our way to a map reference, where we would take part in a mock battle, firing off blank cartridges, our performance being assessed by an officer from the local regiment. We were told by a visiting general that the tactics deployed had not been in use since the Crimean War, a comment of which the headmaster was, without doubt, very proud.

Shrewsbury's political influence had been at its greatest during the reign of James II, but had since waned, with Michael Heseltine being the most noted old Salopian politician of recent years. Charles Darwin was its most famous alumnus but the best known old boys since the 1960s have been satirists such as Richard Ingrams and Willie Rushton, the comedian Michael Palin and disc jockeys such as Simon Dee (Cyril Henty-Dodd) and John Peel (John Ravenscroft). But that Stiff Upper Lip was the presiding ethos of the school was shown in the 1956 Masque written by Paul Dehn to celebrate the four hundredth anniversary of the founding of the School. Though Darwin featured in this, the others included the Elizabethan poet and soldier Sir Philip Sidney who, while lying mortally wounded at the battle of Zutphen in 1586, handed his water bottle to a dying soldier saying 'thy need is greater than mine', Andrew Irvine who died with George Mallory climbing Everest, and an RAF pilot officer, without doubt referring to the Spitfire pilot Richard Hillary who, despite his hands and face being appallingly burnt after he was shot down during the Battle of Britain, insisted on returning to duty, and was lost after his plane crashed in 1943.

These were the people one was meant to live up to at Shrewsbury, my father considering Sir Philip Sidney an especially stirring example of courage and fortitude. But I failed dismally. It was made pretty plain to me in our house, Riggs Hall, that I lacked the qualities that had made these three Old Salopians – drive and initiative. Being called spineless was the ultimate put-down. But if I felt bullied I was to some extent a bully myself, driven by feelings of insecurity. This insecurity was reinforced by the breakdown of my parents' marriage.

Semi-feudal North Shropshire was never going to be an ideal place for my mother. When she started to speak and canvass on behalf of the Labour party, my father's predecessor, Dr Woolward, got in touch to tell him that doctors' wives in Shropshire did not support the Labour Party. If this injunction was resisted it was not for long. Hoping to link up with all the other young women with children in the village, she applied to join the Mothers' Union but, as a divorcee, was rejected by the Vicar. Though a happy, hardworking and resourceful individual, she was left bored and isolated so that over the years a latent anxiety eventually destabilised her.

Unable to deal with this and rebel in any constructive way against the strictures of Shrewsbury School, I took to drink – the traditional family way out – sneaking out to pubs at night. My father could not cope either and one of the worst experiences of my life was the sight of him, after a row with my mother, rushing down the stairs crying and running from the house. It was unbearable to see him, the preacher and practitioner of stoicism, reduced to tears.

As his dreams of an idyllic life in the countryside with his sons following him on as doctors fell apart, he increased his already heavy drinking and ate little. With my mother gone, he drank in pubs and at home – at least a bottle of whisky a day, creeping out at night to hurl the empties into an overgrown part of the garden where nearly 30 years later hundreds were discovered by a Dutch couple who had bought the house. But he would not give up or retire, working right up to his death at 76. His practice declined as he gained no new patients though he retained the loyalty of the older ones, having in the end what another local doctor described as a 'geriatric practice'.

My image of him at this time is of a man desperately and bravely trying to hide his anger, sadness and disappointment. The one lapse into crying on the stairs was never repeated, at least not that I ever saw. And I have a suspicion that even in private he gritted his teeth and bore it, never giving way to the tears that would have relieved the internal gnawing pain. One day in July 1976 he sat at his kitchen table, no doubt adding some whisky to his early morning tea, and opened up a letter containing the results of a test on his sputum which showed that his persistent cough was indeed the tuberculosis he had suspected. In just over a month he was dead. And of course to some extent he got it wrong about the Spartan boy and the fox. Perhaps there is a better lesson to be learnt, that if you don't admit to your pain and anguish you may be eaten away or even consumed internally and of course that is what the tuberculosis, originally called consumption, did to my father.

——ooOoo——

After leaving Shrewsbury School in 1963 at the age of 17, Nick Spurrier held numerous ill paid positions such as petrol pump attendant and dish washer. From 1970-73, he studied history at the London School of Economics. A year spent hitchhiking in Europe, and in Africa, from Tunisia to Malawi, was followed by a successful effort to combat his alcoholism. Bookselling and writing have been his subsequent occupations, with a short period teaching at Canterbury College, Canterbury Prison and Dover Borstal.

THE RUINED MILL

John Sussams

Although he had numerous friends and acquaintances, John was, essentially, a loner. When he was no more than fourteen years old and his contemporaries were all shouting themselves hoarse at football matches, John used to go up onto the Hallamshire Moors, all by himself, with map and compass, exploring. Well, that's what he called it. Actually, what he was doing was familiarising himself with the terrain, so that, within an area of several square miles, he knew every landmark, every track, every pothole, every outcrop of rock, every watercourse, every shepherd's hut, every shooting cabin.

The official Ordnance Survey map was out of date. John's amended version was more accurate. There were things on John's map which, apparently, the Ordnance Survey did not know about ... yet. The recently constructed Ladybower Reservoir was not marked but would doubtless be on the next official OS issue of the map of the area. In the meantime, John had sketched it in on his map. He could understand why some temporary structure, built to shelter a grouse-shooting party from the wind and the rain, might not appear on the official map. But ancient stone circles and tumuli were normally always marked. They had been there for thousands of years. But what about this ruined mill? How long had it been deserted? Fifty years? A hundred years? Longer? Who would know? And why wasn't it marked on the map?

John came upon the mill by chance one Sunday afternoon, having taken a different path from the one he usually took. It was cold and misty. He scrambled down a steep rocky slope until he came to a boggy area which was the source of a small stream. He followed the stream until, about a quarter of a mile further on, it petered out in what looked like another boggy area but what was in fact an almost completely silted up millpond. On the far side could be seen the ruined building which had once been a working mill, and a small area of clear water. John went across to investigate. He peered into the water to see if there were any fish. Apparently not. Marsh gas bubbled up from the depths. The building had collapsed long ago and was overgrown with brambles and elders. The walls were in places a few feet high. Water was seeping out at a lower level and trickling away towards a plantation of pine trees.

John got his map out and studied it. There was The Edge, where the contours on the map all came together to indicate an almost sheer drop of up to two hundred feet; and there was The Plantation, depicted with symbolic rows of trees. Somewhere between the two was the millpond and the mill. But they were not shown on the map. John made a mark on his map and wrote 'Ruined Mill'. Then he thought he would light a fire and went to collect some dry wood from the plantation. Emerging with an armful of sticks, he was surprised to see a man standing by the ruined mill. The man was beckoning him.

'The best place to light a fire would be in this corner, out of the wind, said the man. He was old, with a weather-beaten face and bushy grey sideburns of the type that had been popular a hundred years earlier. He must have been at least seventy, maybe eighty. He was wearing a fawn duffel coat and had no trace of a Yorkshire accent.

'Yes, Sir,' said John.

'I am Alfred J Tunmer,' said the old man, extending his hand, 'currently resident at the George Hotel, Hathersage.'

'I am John C Arthur,' said John, 'currently resident in Collegiate Crescent, Sheffield 10.'

'So, what brings you here?' asked Alfred J Tunmer.

'I like hiking. This place is not marked on the map. Do you know why that is?'

'Probably because the map makers thought it was unimportant. All maps are inaccurate. I know about maps. I have written a book about maps. On your one-inch map the main roads are shown in red and are one-sixteenth of an inch wide. How wide does that suggest they are?'

John paused. 'A hundred and ten yards, I suppose. But …'

'But what?'

'But maps are just to help you find things on the ground. They don't have to show everything, like photographs. They miss out a lot. They use symbols. You could hardly see a road on the map if it were drawn to scale.' John did some rough mental arithmetic. 'The line would be only about five thousandths of an inch wide.'

'Very good, Boy! And there was no room on the map for these ruins. If they were shown on the map, people would look for them and then they wouldn't find them.'

'Why not? I found them didn't I?'

'Yes, but you weren't looking for them, were you?'

John was perplexed by what Alfred J Tunmer was trying to say. What *was* he trying to say? 'Well, I think ruins are very interesting,' John said. 'I mean, if there was a mill here once, there would have been other buildings, maybe a whole village, probably in the Domesday Book.'

'Yes, you are right. There were once fifteen cottages here, a smithy, an alehouse, and a barn, all abandoned long ago. Let me show you.'

John thought the old man was about to produce some crumpled document from his coat pocket. What was he? A geographer? A historian? Or just a lonely old man? As he spoke, the old man's words seemed to conjure up visions of the past. The millpond was clear and deep. Many fish – carp, rudd, roach, and perch – could be seen swimming around. The mill reconstructed itself, the wheel turning slowly in the stream. Buildings arose miraculously from the ground – whitewashed cottages with roofs made of thin slabs of stone. There were horses, cows, numerous chickens and geese, and people, lots of people, going about their daily business, dressed in the manner of two hundred years ago. Sitting on a seat outside the alehouse was an old man. He was talking to a youth. The old man was the spitting image of Alfred J Tunmer. The youth was himself, another John, a doppelganger.

John could not see the real Alfred J Tunmer. Where was he? He could hear his voice, but the voice was inside his head. John suddenly realised that he too was invisible. Well, of course. And the voice inside his head was saying 'You can see them but they can't see you. That's because they are here and you aren't. Or it could be the other way round. You could be here and visible but then they would not be here. They would be invisible.'

The kettle was boiling. It was time for a brew. John looked around. Alfred J Tunmer was nowhere to be seen. Marsh gas bubbled up from the vegetation rotting below the surface of the stagnant pool. The mist was lifting. The song of a blackbird could be heard.

'Huh!' said John out loud. I must be letting my imagination run away with me. Alfred J Tunmer? What kind of name is that?

But he was haunted by the memory of that strange vision. And the very next day he went down to the City Library to see if he could find Alfred J Tunmer's book on maps. It was not in the index. Then he went to see if he could find it in Applebaum's second-hand bookshop. You'd be amazed at what could be found in that emporium if you ferreted around long enough. But on this occasion, John had no luck. *Out and about on Kinderscout* by one Fred J Turner was the best that could be done. The magic words 'with maps' also appeared on the cover of this book. Could Turner that be an alias? Might Tunmer and Turner be one and the same? As well as maps, this whimsical volume also contained 'Directions for finding Kinderlow Cavern' and (John thought) was well worth sixpence. He didn't know there was a Kinderlow Cavern.

A month passed and John decided that it was time to revisit his ruined mill. But he couldn't find it. What was it the old man had said? 'If they [the ruins] were shown on the map, people would look for them and then they wouldn't find them.' John found the exact place on the map – the place which he had marked with a cross and labelled 'Ruined Mill', halfway between the rocky edge and the plantation of pine trees. Here, right where he was standing. But there was no trace of it. No ruins. No boggy place. Nothing. Well, it had not rained for some time, but even so …

John went down to the village and located the George Hotel. He asked the receptionist: 'Do you have an Alfred J Tunmer resident here?'

'Just a minute,' said the receptionist, and she searched through the hotel register. 'No,' she said, 'apparently not.'

'Well, that's funny,' said John. 'Why would he say that he was resident here, if he wasn't?'

'Mrs Bluett!' the receptionist called. 'There's someone here asking for a Mr Alfred Tunmer. Can we help him?'

'Alf Tunmer!' exclaimed Mrs Bluett, the red-faced, somewhat corpulent. middle-aged manageress of the George Hotel. 'Well, yes, we did have an Alfred Tunmer here, a retired geography teacher … but he died over two years ago.'

—ooOoo—

John Sussams was educated at King Edward VII School, Sheffield, and Gonville & Caius College, Cambridge, reading Modern Languages. He has been a writer, off and on, during the whole of his working life in industry and as a management consultant, having published five technical books and numerous articles. After taking early retirement he moved to Folkestone in 1994 and has concentrated on painting and on creative writing. He has published three novels and a number of short stories.

ELECTRONIC WARFARE

Alexander Tulloch

Major Hicks (Rtd), ex- Royal Signals, stood back from his workbench, took a sip of coffee and surveyed his handiwork. He had spent the last four Saturday mornings shut away in the garage of his suburban semi, tinkering with his son's discarded ghettoblaster and now, he hoped, the job was finished. His secret weapon was ready to be put to the test.

It was not without a certain trepidation and a vague feeling of excitement mixed with apprehension that he placed his empty coffee cup on the shelf behind him and then gingerly moved his hand towards the 'ON' switch. Time seemed to stand still as he turned the knob and waited. Finally he was able to breathe a sigh of relief as the realisation dawned on him that he had not been wasting his time. All his calculations and intuitive hunches had proved right because what came out of the mighty twin speakers was........nothing......absolutely nothing.....not a sound. He then turned his invention off in preparation for the next stage of the operation even though, in his heart of hearts, he was convinced that from now on there would be no hitches, no gremlins and that his redesigned ghettoblaster would work as he had hoped and predicted.

The feverish activity of the past few Saturday mornings had not been brought about by some sudden whim, nor was it the result of some crackpot idea dreamed up by some dotty professor languishing in the bath. No, not at all. Major Archibald Hicks (Rtd) was a man with his feet firmly on the ground. He had no illusions about what was possible and what was not. But the idea of constructing a radio which would broadcast silence and suppress all sounds in the immediate vicinity had been lurking in the darker recesses of his imagination since his time with the army in the Falklands. It had been a noisy war and, although the major had come through physically unscathed, the exploding bombs, rockets and shells, and the almost interminable chatter of the Browning heavy machine guns had left their psychological imprint. As soon as the enemy's surrender at Port Stanley was announced a noticeable change came over the major and he found that his tolerance threshold to noise nose-dived. He could no longer stand to be in a crowded pub or noisy department store and the mere thought of an approaching Dinner Night in the Officers' Mess was enough to fill him with dread. In fact, it is no exaggeration to say that when he was offered the opportunity for early retirement, the seductive prospect of spending most of his time in quieter surroundings was, in all probability, the deciding factor.

The moment when he finally switched on the redesigned ghettoblaster, then, was a moment of paramount importance for him. It signalled the end of the tyranny of noise and the beginning of a time when he could be master of his own little universe, a universe which, at the touch of a button, could be completely free of the cacophonous barrage which had assailed his every waking moment for more years than he cared to remember. If things went according to plan, and the major was certain that they would, the television, the washing machine, lawnmower, next door's motorbike and his son's stereo would no longer be capable of awakening suicidal tendencies in him. So with his revamped ghettoblaster slung over his shoulder and his fingers firmly crossed he set off down the road to see if his high hopes were to be justified.

As he approached the bus stop his heart leaped. There, waiting for the number 29 which would take them into the town centre, stood two middle-aged women in their regulation plastic macs and head scarves. From twenty feet away the major sensed that they would be perfect guinea pigs for the first stage of the experiment. He knew from experience that it is simply impossible for two women to stand at a bus stop and not gossip. The closer he got to them the clearer he could hear their voices as they nattered on, each trying to outdo the other with the juiciness of their own little snippets of scandal. Louder and louder their voices seemed to get as he walked up to them and pretended to take his place in the queue. Once stationed strategically behind them he turned away slightly so that they would not see as he surreptitiously let his hand slide down to the 'ON' switch and turned it. The effect was immediate. The two women began to stare at each other in amazement. Neither could understand what was happening. Their jaws continued to mouth complete sentences, but no sound left their lips. 'It works!' thought Archibald, scarcely able to contain himself, 'It works! And that's with the volume set at minimum!'

He turned it off just in time to catch one of the women mid-sentence as she said [… God! Mabel, I thought I'd gone deaf for a moment then, or you'd been struck dumb. I couldn't hear a thing!'

Satisfied, not to say elated, with this initial success the major now decided that a larger scale experiment would be in order. He therefore deftly about-turned and, pacing along like a smart young recruit on the parade ground, set a course for the local pub.

Once through the doors he knew instinctively that he was in an ideal place for what he was about to do. The noise was horrendous. There were people shouting across the bar for their pints, others laughing uproariously, no doubt in response to some smutty story one of their number had just recounted and yet others were singing their heads off to the accompaniment of a raucous pop song belting out of the jukebox.

'Perfect,' the major said to himself as he sat down on a stool at the end of the bar. 'Now let's see what happens here.'

Not wishing to overdo things straightaway he turned the ghettoblaster on, but once again kept the volume to a minimum. The effect was exactly the same as at the bus stop. The barmaid, standing on the other side of the bar and not two feet away from the major, was exchanging a few pleasantries with a middle-aged man as she handed him his double Irish. Suddenly a look of astonishment flashed across their faces as their flow of words came to an abrupt halt. They both knew that they were talking and, theoretically at least, should have been able to hear each other, but they could not. Words should have flowed from their lips, but they did not. Both, therefore, assumed that they had been smitten by instantaneous deafness.

'Wonderful!' thought the major. 'Now let's see what this beauty is really capable of!'

At the far end of the bar a group of men were watching the horse-racing on the television. Shouts of joy and despair erupted as the winners and losers heard the result of a photo-finish confirmed by the booming voice of the commentator. Slowly, so as not to attract anyone's attention, he let his hand slide down once more to the 'ON' switch; but this time he was not going to pussyfoot about with the minimum volume. This time it was going to be a full-scale, head-on, all-out attack. The enemy was out there and the major had decided that he was not in the business of taking prisoners. There would be only one loser in this battle and Archibald Hicks had resolved that it was not going to be him.

The ghettoblaster worked a treat. Forty watts of silence blasted the whole room and completely overwhelmed the dreadful din which, under normal circumstances, would have been sufficient cause for him not to want to come within a mile of the place. Not a whisper could be heard, not a sound detected and even the normally ubiquitous drone of the traffic was unable to penetrate the dense wall of beautiful silence with which the major had flooded the pub.

Now that he knew his invention worked he felt he should switch it off and go home. But a little voice inside his head persuaded him not to rush off just yet: the entertainment was just too good to miss. A somewhat impish enjoyment had crept up on him as he sat there watching the antics of the pub's regulars as they tried to come to terms with sudden, inexplicable deafness. The scene being enacted before the mischievous major's eyes was like something out of a silent movie in which arms wave excessively, lip movements and bodily gestures are exaggerated beyond belief. He, on the other hand, wallowed in the sensual symphony of silence as he turned to enjoy the first 'quiet pint' he had had in years. Victory was not just sweet, it was positively intoxicating.

What the major had not bargained for was the panic which the total silence was to cause among the regulars at the Dog and Gun. Some of them began poking their fingers in their ears, others took to thumping the sides of their heads with the heels of their hands and yet others clasped their throats as they frantically attempted to reactivate their vocal cords. When they realised that everyone in the pub had been struck by this mysterious affliction panic developed into out-and-out hysteria. Tables were knocked over, glasses were spilled as everyone tried to get out, believing, as they did, that once outside their hearing would be restored. Even the major began to think that he had, perhaps, taken things a little too far and, in any case, he could hardly just sit there, enjoying a quiet pint surrounded by such silent pandemonium. So he decided that it was time to declare a truce and to switch the silence off. No sooner had 'normal service' been resumed than one elderly man made a bayonet charge for him straight across the bar.

' 'Ere you!' he spluttered. 'I've been watching you. I don't understand 'ow you did it, but you made everything in 'ere go quiet. And it's got something to do with that funny wireless you've got there. I saw your 'and move to the knob and then we was all struck mutt'n'jeff. Got a bloody cheek you 'ave, mate. I came in 'ere to 'ave a couple o' pints and pick my gee-gees for the 3 o'clock at Sandown, an' you come in an' mess things up. 'Ow's a feller supposed to concentrate on the form with all that bleedin' silence goin' on? Go on, bloody well clear off out of it!'

This, it seemed to the major, was a good time to effect a tactical withdrawal. After all, who was he to contradict the time-honoured maxim about discretion being the better part of valour. And surely an orderly retreat would be infinitely preferable to a bloody rout or, at the very least, a severe mauling by the enemy, either of which, his antennae were telling him, was a distinct possibility if he stayed much longer.

He therefore picked up his portable engine of war and moved off confidently towards the door. As he was walking through it he heard someone shout, as a parting shot, ' ... and bloody good riddance!' before it swung shut and cut him off from what was probably a choice selection of a few more vernacular expressions.

Once outside Major Archibald Hicks, (Rtd). took a deep breath. It was not the first time in his military career that he had been on the winning side, but this time was different. This time he had planned the whole campaign himself, executed it with military precision and acquired the power not merely to defeat the enemy but also to annihilate him at the turn of a switch. The euphoria of victory flowed through his veins and put the ramrod back into his spine as he strode along the high street. Unfortunately for Major Hicks (Rtd). the ecstatic state produced by such a brilliant military success made him forgetful of his highway code and he stepped off the pavement right into the path of an oncoming roaring, snorting beast of a motorbike. The last thing he saw before losing consciousness was a missile, which looked uncannily like his wonderful ghettoblaster, flying through the air and exploding into a thousand pieces of shrapnel against the gable-end of the butcher's shop opposite.

When he opened his eyes he saw that his left leg and arm were both in plaster and he simultaneously became aware of what felt like several layers of bandages around his head. So he knew he was in hospital. He raised his head a little and could just make out the outlines of two people, obviously deep in conversation, on the other side of the curtain which surrounded his bed. Had he been able to hear them, he would have heard the educated, clipped speech of the consultant who was saying ' … yes, Mrs Hicks, your husband will live and his bones will soon mend. Unfortunately, however, his head injuries are such that we think it's more than likely that he will be profoundly deaf.'

—ooOoo—

THE VISITOR

Alexander Tulloch

'Hello.'
'Hello. Who are you?'
'Death.'
'You mean your name is Death? Isn't it usually pronounced De'Ath?'
'It may be, but I wasn't telling you my surname. I am Death. You know, as in "popped his clogs" or "fell off his perch" and I have come for you.'
'What? You can't be serious. I'm too young and there's nothing wrong with me. I'm perfectly healthy, very fit even.'
'Yes, I know. But that doesn't make any difference. When it's time to go, it's time to go. I've had my orders and so I've come for you.'
'Wait a minute. I must be dreaming. You're just a figment of my imagination.'

'Technically speaking, part of what you say is true. But only part of it. You are dreaming in the sense that you are at this moment lying on the couch enjoying a nap after a splendid Sunday lunch. Your children are on the floor watching TV (you do watch some rubbish, don't you?) and your wife's trying to read the newspaper but your snoring is disturbing her. But never mind, that'll soon stop and she'll be able to read in peace.'

'Now listen. I'm forty-one years old and still in my prime. I have no medical problems and, as I've already said, I'm very fit. I play squash twice a week and football on Sunday mornings. If you really are who you say you are, why don't you go and find some ninety-year-old or someone suffering from some painful, incurable disease. They probably wouldn't object and may even welcome a visit from you.'

'Sorry. I understand your arguments very well, but there's nothing I can do about it. I have my quota to fill. I've already taken away some old folk this morning and a few not so old who had incurable illnesses. Now I have to take a few young, fit people.'

'But why? Why do you have to take young, fit people?'

'For the football team.'

'Say that again. I think I misheard you.'

'I said I've come to take you because we need you for the football team.'

'That's what I thought you said. Are you telling me that in the afterlife you have football teams?'

'Of course. Why not? You have them in this life, so why shouldn't we have them?'

'I'm sorry but all this is going to take a bit of getting used to. We're told that after death we either go to Heaven or Hell. In the former we get bored to death ...sorry, I'll rephrase that.......we lead a very uneventful life, just sitting on a cloud all day playing a harp. In the other place it's all fire and brimstone and endless pain and torture. What you've just said doesn't really fit in with that picture.'

'I'm not surprised. Whoever told you that had no idea what he was talking about. It's true that there are two, shall we say, "departments" The place you refer to as "Heaven" is for the boring old sods who make everyone's life down here a misery by filling their heads with meaningless propaganda about "eternal torture" and "fire and brimstone". What you call "Hell" is only for people who have a spark of life in them (please excuse the pyrotechnical allusion) and, believe me, life there is never boring.'

'I'm very glad to hear it. But it still doesn't mean I'm in a hurry to go there. There are still too many things I want to- do here and lots of places I want to visit.'

'Look, I've told you. Nothing you say will make me change my mind. Your time is up and we need you for our football team. The Inter-Stellar Cup eliminator rounds start next week and you've been selected. We didn't do very well last time the competition was held. So you're being brought in to give us a better chance.'

'But this is ridiculous. Are you saying that I'm going to die just because you want to increase your chances in some stupid football competition?'

'Stupid? Did you say stupid? How can you say that about the Inter-Stellar Cup? I'll have you know that it's a great honour to be even considered for a place in the team, let alone chosen as you are. We have some very good players and you should be proud to be selected to join their ranks.'

'Oh, yes? Some good players? Name some.'

'Well, let me see now, yes, there's Hitler, the striker, and Stalin who plays half-back. The captain's name is da Vinci. He used to paint pictures and dabble in science when he was down here. God! Can he run when he gets the ball! My only criticism of him is that he tends to spend a bit too much time drawing up elaborate plans to illustrate tactics. It all gets a bit involved and he talks way above the heads of the other players. He assumes everybody else is as clever as he is, but of course they aren't. Hitler and Stalin are pretty good, too. Very good at doing the unexpected.

The only problem with them is that they both refuse to play by the book and keep getting sent off for fouls. Then there's Churchill, the goalie. On a good day nothing gets past him, but he does take a long time to "warm up" and he drives the other players mad by insisting on smoking those damn cigars, even during a match! The best of them all, though, is Robin Hood. A right little tear-away he is when he wants to be. You should have seen him last week in the friendly. He and Hitler ran rings round the opposition. We'd have won if that twit Caesar hadn't cocked things up by scoring two own goals. Caesar and Alexander the Great always spend most of the match trying to outdo each other. I'm actually seriously thinking of dropping one of them when I decide which of them is more expendable. I might bring Napoleon on in place of Caesar, the only trouble is that with one arm constantly tucked into his jacket his balance isn't as good as it might be. I have thought of putting him on the right wing to counterbalance Nelson on the left. The trouble there, though, is that Nelson and Wellington are dynamite together and if I bring Boney in they might start re-enacting the Napoleonic Wars and that wouldn't be good for morale. I'm sure you understand that, being a good team-player yourself.'

'Well, yes, I suppose I do see your point. But why don't you leave all this to the manager to sort out?'

'I **am** the manager! It's what you might call one of my secondary duties. My primary duty, as you see, is to collect those souls who are due to come to us. It's just a happy coincidence that I can combine the 'corpse run' with my interest in football. Anyway, are you ready now? I can't stand here all day talking to you; I've several more calls to make and there's a practice session tonight and I mustn't be late for it.'

'But I don't want to go. I refuse to go. You could at least give me a bit more time here. I have all sorts of things to sort out before I die. You know the sort of things I mean: insurance policies, VAT returns, income tax forms. I can't just go and leave my wife to sort that lot out.'

'Sorry, your time is up and you're coming with me.'
'Over my dead body!'
'Precisely.'
'I'm not going!'
'Look. Let's get things clear. You don't have any say in the matter. The moment I snap my fingers your existence down here will be over and you will find yourself in another place. There's no time to lose because you have to get all kitted out for the big match and get some training in. Then there's the question of your football boots. You'll need a few days to get a new pair broken in. So come on, have a last look at your family and we'll be off.'

'Wait! Wait! I have another question.'
'What is it now?'
'Well, it occurs to me that all those team members you mentioned before (you know, Hitler, Napoleon and the others) - they're all famous people. I'm not famous. How would I fit in with that lot?'

'No problem at all. I only mentioned a few of the squad members. The only other famous name we have is William Shakespeare.'

'William Shakespeare! What good is he? He was just a baldy playwright!'

'That's got nothing to do with it. He may have been a baldy old playwright down here, but now he's one of our best wingers. And while we're on the subject, I might just mention that our best writers up there are Dixie Dean and Bobby Moore."

'Writers? You mean you have books in the after-life?'
'Of course we do. And libraries, newspapers, art galleries, pubs, restaurants, athlete's foot and income tax.'

'Income tax? Are you telling me now that the bloody tax man follows us even after the grave?'

'Of course. You surely didn't think you could escape taxes just by dying, did you? That would be far too easy. The tax inspectors and bank managers are actually some of the most active members of our society. They follow people around just as they did down here. The difference is that, unlike when they were on earth, they are the jolliest people of all because they know that their quarry can't be so unsporting as to die and avoid paying their debts. Now they can pursue people for all eternity and milk them dry with even greater gusto. But of course they're not in the football team. One or two of them have expressed an interest in playing, but if I allowed them to join the team everyone else would resign. Then I'd have to start all over again and form a team comprised solely of bankers and tax inspectors and not even I could stand working with that lot all the time. Have you ever noticed how you can never have a decent conversation with them about anything but money? You start talking about tactics and somehow they always bring the conversation round to house prices, negative equity, stocks and shares etc. I don't know how they manage it but they do and it drives me up the wall. But listen, I haven't got time to talk to you like this. I've told you, I'm in a hurry and it's time for you to come with me. Stop delaying matters and playing for time.'

'What do you expect me to do? I don't want to go with you. Nothing you have said (which, I admit, is all very interesting, not to mention surprising) makes me think that I would not rather stay here. My wife's too young to be left a widow and I want to see my kids grow up and, hopefully, see my grandchildren. So why don't you just go and leave me in peace. I was enjoying this little nap before you appeared and I still think you're just a bad dream and that when I wake up I'll be able to just take the dog for a walk and have a relaxing smoke. Then I'll get everything back into perspective and convince myself that you're nothing more than the result of eating too much cheese after lunch.'

;Smoke? Did you say you would go for a smoke?'

'Yes. You're not going to start lecturing me on that now, are you?'

'No. But I didn't know you were a smoker. There's nothing in my records to say that you smoke cigarettes. I'll have something to say to my research department when I get back.'

'Why, what's wrong? Is there some problem?"

'Well, yes, there is. There have been so many protests about Churchill and Stalin smoking that the new club rules stipulate quite categorically that no smokers or even ex-smokers can be recruited into the squad.'

'Does that mean you can't use me then?'

'Well, yes, I'm afraid it does. It looks like I can't take you with me now after all. Oh dear, I've wasted all this time coming here and talking to you. But I'll be back for you some day.'

'**COFFEE..........JOHN.........DO YOU WANT THIS COFFEE?**'

'What?........Oh, yes. Thanks'

'You were so fast asleep I thought you were dead."

'Well, er.......yes........I was dead to the world. Oh good, coffee. Can you pass me my fags?'

'Here. When are you going to stop smoking those filthy things? You know they're bad for you. Doesn't it bother you that smoking is bad for the heart? You could just fall asleep on that couch one day and never wake up.'

——ooOoo——

Alexander Tulloch is a retired Senior Lecturer in Russian and Spanish. He worked with the MoD for many years and was latterly responsible for training interpreters in specialist reserve units. He has published translations of some of the classics in Spanish and Russian literature as well as several books of his own, including two on Liverpool, two on Kent and one on the origin of everyday words in English. He is also a Fellow of the Institute of Linguists.

TELL HIM NOW

Mike Umbers

The caravan had been Steve's idea. Shelley knew why, and he knew she knew – they'd never slept together! Lots of quickies, at her house when Mum was at Bingo, or in the woods behind the Army Ranges, often uncomfortably and always against the clock and never all night. She teased him about the van, but of course she wanted it too. He'd borrowed it from his mate Geoff, got a 72-hour pass, and she'd taken the Friday off. They'd borrowed a duvet from Sis, and stopped off at Tesco for food, and arrived at the site on Geoff's farm about 3.30, and she'd been arranging things in the tiny kitchen while he did unnecessary things to his precious car – she could see him now through the window, polishing it. She laughed affectionately: this was like two kids playing house, the difference was what would happen later.

All the time though, at the back of her mind, she was waiting for Sis. If the Result came today Sis would find it when she got home from work; that would be any time now – they'd given Sis's address so an official NHS envelope wouldn't land on Mum's mat, because she'd want to know what was going on. Mum thought she was spending the weekend with Sis; of course she'd had to tell Sis, and Sis had been a bit sniffy about it, especially when she heard Steve was a soldier: soldiers hadn't too good a reputation in Colchester. Besides, Sis and David had been trying for two years so you could understand she was a bit jealous.

But she gave good advice: if you are, she said, tell him at the right moment and say something like 'I'm going to have your baby,' not just 'I'm pregnant,' so he knows it's his problem as well as yours.

But when was the right moment? That's what she kept asking herself. She was filling the kettle from the plastic water can when her phone jangled, and she jumped even though she'd been half expecting it. She pressed it.

'Positive', the text read. 'Tell him now like we said. XXX'

She stared at it. She'd known, somehow, but even so it was a shock. She texted back 'OK' and deleted everything. Tell him now? He might walk out, simply drive away. No, he wouldn't leave her here, but he might drive her home in frozen silence. Or he might be angry with her, as if it were her fault. Suppose he said 'Get rid of it' – she couldn't bear that – she wanted his baby – her baby – even if she lost him, and so would her Mum who was desperate for Sis to produce and kept dropping painful hints. She realised she didn't know him very well. Not the important things about him. They'd never discussed families, but he'd told Geoff a bit, and Geoff had told her that his father had walked out on his Mum when Steve was little, and that his Mum drank and had a boyfriend he hated, but he'd never opened up to her about all that. And she knew he'd been in care as a teenager and that he'd joined the Army as soon as he was old enough, and loved it, especially the sport, and having enough money for a decent car and to take a girl out. And she'd been the girl, for the last 18 months anyway. And he wasn't the typical soldier type Sis probably thought he was – he was kind and thoughtful, and not just 'after one thing'. They'd kissed a bit and cuddled a bit from the start, as you do, but it was only in the last three months that they'd made love properly, and it was proper tender loving not just sex, well, she thought so anyway, and she'd wanted it as much as him, though she'd never done it with anyone else, and he was the experienced one, and he'd been so gentle and so caring afterwards that she felt she could trust him. But could she trust him now this had happened?

She made the tea and called Steve in and they sat side by side on the bench seat to drink it, facing the little TV Geoff had put in for them specially. He put his arm round her shoulder. 'This is nice,' he said stretching his legs out. 'Like kids playing house. You know Geoff and Sue used to live in here? Before her Dad died and they moved into the farmhouse. He warned me about bouncing too hard – the whole van rocks. We're on the bed now, do you know that? It pulls out, there's a handle under here.' She laughed. 'Are you wanting to open it now, or will that wait until we've eaten? We've all that food to get through, remember?' 'Yeah, it'll wait till then. We can take our time – we've all night for once. It's like living together at home.' She heard a sudden seriousness in his tone, a slight emphasis on 'home': if Geoff was right he'd not had a proper family home since he was a kid when his Dad left. Surely this was the moment to tell him, while he was feeling sort of romantic and sentimental? But perhaps it wasn't? Wouldn't it be better in bed, lying close and intimate, afterwards? She hesitated, and the moment was gone, his thoughts were off, planning the weekend. 'We'll drive to Mersea tomorrow, and picnic on the beach if it's nice. Ever had oysters? They sell them there. Oh, and Geoff said call on them teatime tomorrow, and say hello to Sue and her Mum. We must thank Sue – she cleaned the caravan up and got it ready for us. Should we take her something?'

    She wouldn't let him help get the meal; so he opened a beer and watched TV and made comments about the programme. What fun he was to be with. If only this wasn't hanging over her. He enjoyed the food, helped wash up and put away, then organised the bed and spread the duvet. It was only 9 o'clock, but they both wanted to get close, get the van rocking. Watching TV didn't appeal somehow – once he'd seen the football results, anyway. Afterwards she pressed against him feeling his heart pounding and knew it wasn't the moment. When they woke, that would be the best time, so as not to spoil their first night together ... But when she woke Steve was already up, looking for dishes for the cornflakes and boiling water to make tea and she realised he wasn't used to home life but with his Army training he could perfectly well look after himself. She sighed – it would have to be on the beach. This couldn't go on. Every hour that passed made it harder to say.

And on the beach it was: they took off tops and socks and trainers, and lay in the warm sun in the shadow of a groyne. Steve was too active to lie for long though; he sat up and was throwing stones at a marker until she pulled him down to her side. 'Steve, I want to say something….' 'Mmm?' 'I had a text from my sister. It's my test result – I'm going to have our baby, Steve.' There! Done! After all that waiting and worrying, it took one minute and two sentences. And 'our baby', not 'your baby'. Surely that was better. He sat up violently, twisting towards her. 'You can't be, I've always …' 'But it burst, didn't it? That night at my place when Mum was out.' He'd forgotten that; he'd rolled away at once and she'd gone off to get vinegar and run a bath and he'd skulked off back to Camp. She'd not mentioned it again; he'd really forgotten it had happened, though he'd been more careful since. She didn't say anything more; it was his turn. But he didn't speak either. He stood up quickly, his expression unfathomable, and walked quickly away from her down the beach in bare feet, apparently ignoring the stones. She sat up and watched him go, unable to read his thoughts from his retreating back, and wanting to call out after him but somehow not daring to, her mouth dry and her body trembling and longing for his comfort and not knowing if she would ever get it.

Steve walked to the water's edge. He couldn't focus his thoughts, but he was crying. Crying! Him, Steve Hughes, Private First Class, Machine Gunner, 1 Section, 4 Platoon, Company Soccer Captain. He felt in his back pocket and pulled out his wallet; in the back bit was a photo, torn and creased. He looked at it trying to focus: his father in their back garden, himself holding a football in a 'We are the Champions' pose, his mother had been on it but he'd torn her off. He was seven. Just before Dad left. Mam had gone to pieces then – drinking; they'd had to move to that awful flat – no garden there – and she'd taken up with Pete, and Pete had ... he couldn't say even to himself what Pete had done; but when Pete had finally broken Mam's arm the Police and the Social had been round and he'd shopped him, told them everything, and Pete had gone inside and he'd been taken into care and Mam into Rehab, which never was going to work, but it didn't matter, because he went to the Home and at sixteen-and-a-half into the Juniors at Shorncliffe, and then to the Battalion, and now he'd got the life he wanted, including getting it off with a girl. And the girl was Shelley. Shelley! He turned to look at her: she was sitting as he'd left her, just sitting, looking very alone. And pregnant.

Pregnant. What was he going to say to her? Or do about it? He'd put a girl up the stick; the lads would snigger. But suppose he loved her? He wondered if he did? He told her he did when they made love but perhaps that was the excitement of the moment? She was a lot of fun, and a nice person, looked good, and his baby was inside her. A baby. A boy? Teach him football, go to matches with him, like he had with his Dad. A girl? He'd always wanted a sister, and he'd asked Mam for one when he was little, and she just said she couldn't have any more babies, which he couldn't understand – they'd had him hadn't they? He had a vision of a little blue-eyed girl with fair hair like Shelley's, sticking out in bunches. But admitting to being a father, facing her Mum and her fearsome Sister he'd never met, and having to find a place to live, and splitting his money, and giving up his car – giving up his car! No room for a kid in the back of his lovely sports car that even the officers admired. Could he get a Married Quarter? He'd turned down a chance of training for a lance-jack tape but that would have meant more money, perhaps full corporal later, and promotion meant more points to qualify for a Quarter… Living in a Quarter, coming 'home' to Shelley and his kids every night – no more nights out with the lads. A dream? Or a nightmare, a life sentence?

It wasn't what he'd planned. But he hadn't planned anything really – just thought life would continue, money in the bank every month, bigger and better car, soccer on Saturdays, getting off with a girl, some girl, any girl. Any girl, or Shelley? And Shelley had landed him in a whole new world of responsibility. Could he face that? It was all too sudden, and he wasn't ready.

Steve turned round and walked slowly back up the beach. He could see the Mustang parked on the road behind her; which did he want most? What could he say to her?

Shelley saw him coming, his face set and serious. She couldn't move or speak. He stood at her feet and leaned forward over her. The silence seemed to last for hours, but at last she heard his voice.

'What 'we going to call it, Shell?'

——ooOoo——

HER NEW GATEPOST

Mike Umbers

It was a lovely day for it, the sun really warm already. She'd bought the sand and cement and some matching bricks, and now made a start, stacking the bricks in the drive, hitting the used ones with Daddy's pointed trowel to get the hardened mortar off – she still used all his tools, and Mummy's things too; the house wasn't changed at all. Concentrating, she was barely conscious of a car driving past slowly, then stopping and a door slamming.

'Hello Miss, what you up to?'

When they called her 'Miss' like that they were former pupils of course – she was always seeing them. It was a small town where everyone knew everyone. She looked up. Usually she didn't even remember their names when they came up to her in Tesco or somewhere, and showed off their partners and their babies. She remembered this one though – a young man now, still blond, with startlingly blue eyes, she'd always liked him.

'Hello Christopher,' she said.

He must be 20 now, he'd been in her class for two years, always cheerful, good at games, totally stupid academically, and left at 16. She'd wanted to help him simply because he was an attractive kid. Now he was an attractive young man. Still that fair hair and those smiley eyes. He'd filled out too, as you'd expect, he was now tall and well-built. He was wearing decent denim shorts and a clean T-shirt, and beyond him along the road she saw his car which was at least better than a banger. She'd no car herself, she'd sold Daddy's when he died; no use for it, she cycled to School and the shops. She hoped Christopher had a job, so many she met now didn't, and he'd no qualifications except his looks.

'Some bastard backed into my gatepost. Doing a repair job.' She used 'bastard' self-consciously, but deliberately too, to show him she was treating him as an adult, the old classroom relationship forgotten, they were on new terms. He was a man; when had she last talked to a young man?

He eyed the site and assessed the work involved. 'You can't do that on your own,' he said. 'You don't know me, I'm pretty practical. I do all my own DIY.' He picked up the bolster and club hammer. 'I'll give you a hand.'

'No Chris!' (That was new too: he'd always been Christopher.) 'It's your Saturday and … '

'I'll work all day for twenty quid' he said simply.

'It's a deal. I'll labour for you then.' It was worth that to keep him in her drive. He took over the site, demolishing the smashed gatepost and cleaning and stacking the used bricks neatly while she brought water out in the watering can and did a mix of sand and cement on the garage floor. He watched her circling the heap, pouring water into the centre and turning the dry mix inwards with the shovel until it was the right consistency.

'That's cool,' he said grinning and obviously impressed.

'You've never seen a girl do this I suppose?' she said to him, and to herself she said 'Girl? Who'm I kidding?'

He used the trowel to put a good dollop of her mix on the mortar board and carried it to the end of the drive. 'Perfect!' he said, chopping across it with the trowel. She felt a thrill of pleasure at his praise. He laid the first four bricks to make a square and she saw he knew what he was doing.

'Is this your job, building?' she asked him, wanting to find out more about his life.

'Not now. I did, a bit ago, but I'm gardening now, for the Council. It's a living, I really want to get my HGV Licence, like my Dad. It costs though.' Gardening. She did her own gardening, as she did everything for herself, her small neat garden perfectly organised, not a weed in sight; could she think of something he could do there for her, get him to come back and work here again?

It was warm in the sunshine and he took off his T-shirt, and knelt to lay the first brick of the second layer, overlapping the first. His body was muscular, slightly brown, with a haze of bleached hair down the arms and on his sturdy legs, and across his strong chest, she saw, when he turned to reload the trowel. There was nothing now she could do to help.

'I'll do a drink,' she said, 'Coffee? Tea? Squash?'

'Squash, please, it's warm work.'

She tore herself away and went in through the front door. She looked thoughtfully in the fridge wishing she had beer to offer him. She was no drinker but there were two bottles of white wine in the cupboard under the stairs she'd bought for some occasion ages ago. She slid a bottle into the fridge, made the squash and took it outside. She held it out and he took it without standing up; their fingers touched momentarily round the glass. 'Thanks.' He drank it straight down and put the glass on the brick pile.

She had another idea now: 'Chris, I can't do much more to help. Would you mind if I brought my sketch pad out? You look …' The word on her lips was 'manly' or even 'masculine', but somehow she couldn't use it to him, and she ended weakly 'You look great, kneeling there in the sunlight. Make a good picture.'

He stopped working and looked round at her. 'You used to do that in the playground at Chapel Street; you showed me what you'd done once – a tiny picture of us kids playing … and the trees down by the railway line.'

'I still do it, it's a hobby. Water colours mainly, when I've time.' In fact there was always time, plenty of time …Now she set up in the shade of the garage and he got on with the brick-laying. She used ink for speed. She could put a colour wash over it later and bring out the flesh-tone and the red contrast of the gatepost, now four layers high.

By half past twelve he'd only two layers to go. 'How'll we finish the top?' he asked suddenly, his voice interrupting her concentration.

'I was going to fill the inside with all the debris and put a curved top on. Will there be enough mortar for that?'

'Yeah, just about. But it ought to stand a bit before we fill it, to harden. Once it starts to suck, it'll hold.' She wasn't familiar with the term but understood the meaning.

'We'll stop then, and have a bite to eat and you can fill it in after.'

He put on the last layers and carefully covered the remaining mortar with the empty plastic sand-bag before coming down to the garage and standing close behind her to see her work. 'Hey, that *is* good,' he said, obviously genuinely admiring it, and surprised as non-artists are, that anyone could reproduce a living scene on flat paper.

'I'll finish it after and add some colour; I'll need you to kneel down again. Let's go in and eat. I can do oven chips with eggs and bacon. How's that?'

'M'm, that'll be great.'

She carried the sketchbook and he followed her in, bringing his shirt and the glass. 'Can I go to the toilet, please,' he said, and the school formula made her smile, half expecting him to have his hand up.

'Top of the stairs, use the red towel.' She put the drawing to dry in the sun on the window ledge in the sitting room and went into the kitchen. She heard the toilet flush and a few moments later he came down, his shirt on and hands clean. She pointed to the table. 'You sit at the back and we can talk while I get it ready.'

The last person to sit there had been Daddy. Since then, apart from the Doctor and the Ambulance men, no one had even come into the house, let alone sat at her table. She moved deftly – organised in her own kitchen.

'Are you still at Chapel Street,' he asked. 'Any changes there?'

She considered. Nothing much changed, ever. 'The railway line's been taken up of course. More coloured children – they don't all speak English either.' Then to keep him talking she asked him where he lived.

'Still with Mum and Dad. But we're going to have to move.'

'Why's that?'

'Not room for us all. My partner's pregnant.' He said it half proudly, half regretfully, not at all ashamedly. 'Don't blame her, it was my fault.'

She concentrated on the frypan, moving the bacon round, resolutely keeping her mind free of images. He went on talking. 'She's gone to see her Gran today. You probably knew her, Sarah Bowling? Everyone called her Sally. In Mrs Baker's class.' She had an instant vision of a tall girl with a loud laugh and already showing busty growth. 'No, don't remember her,' she said shortly and put the plate down in front of him, then her own and sat down.

They ate in silence and as soon as he'd finished she stood up and said 'Let's get on. I don't want to keep you all day.'

He stood up. 'Thanks for the food,' he said, 'and thanks for the chance to earn a bit. We really need it now, an' I've got to find lodgings as well, an' get a deposit together.'

She didn't answer and went outside to inspect the brickwork while he followed.

The sun had gone off the drive. He kept his shirt on now, and worked to pack the inside of the column he'd built with all the rubble and old mortar. Finally while she took in her painting things he put a neat dome of cement to finish the top just like the other side. They cleaned up the site together, without need for talk. She collected her tools, and rinsed them under the outside tap while he swept up with the yard broom; she went inside and got two £10 notes, put them in an envelope and wrote Christopher on it. He was ready to go now, standing at the top of the drive; she handed the envelope to him holding one end and he took the other and said 'Thanks. I'll come again if you need anything doing.'

'Thank you,' she said shortly.

He hesitated for a second then walked off back to his car. She didn't watch him go, just shut the garage door and went into the house. She closed the front door and drew the bolt as well; she wasn't going out and no one was coming. She went up to the toilet looking sharply round but there was no sign of his invasion; he'd put the seat down and even left the basin clean. There were no marks on the red towel. She put it for washing anyway. Then she went downstairs and picked up the drawing, quite dry now. She shut the sketchbook without looking at it and slid it back in the sideboard drawer. Then she went into the kitchen and methodically cleared the table, washed up, dried, put away and wiped down. Everything was quite restored to its normal order. Well, almost everything.

She opened the fridge and took out the chilled bottle of wine and replaced it in the cupboard under the stairs next to its fellow. She pushed the little shaped door to. The latch snapped shut with a click.

——ooOoo——

Mike Umbers read English at Trinity Hall, Cambridge, then unexpectedly became a career Soldier. He was posted to Hythe in 1983 and developed an interest in local history, so edited (i.e. wrote!) the Civic Society Newsletter for ten years and produced a commemorative book on Saltwood in 2007. He now contributes regular historical articles for the Saint Leonard's Church Parish Review. Late in life he has turned to fiction: short stories and a novel in first draft.